RESCUED BY A MILLIONAIRE

BY

MARION LENNOX

 MILLS & BOON®

First published in Great Britain 2005
Large Print edition 2005
Harlequin Mills & Boon Limited,
Eton House, 18-24 Paradise Road,
Richmond, Surrey TW9 1SR

© Marion Lennox 2005

ISBN 0 263 18608 3

Set in Times Roman 15 on 17½ pt.
16-1205-55059

Printed and bound in Great Britain
by Antony Rowe Ltd, Chippenham, Wiltshire

RESCUED BY A
MILLIONAIRE

PROLOGUE

His overwhelming sensation was relief.

Wasn't he supposed to feel fury? Desolation? Bitterness? That was what he'd felt in the past when people he loved had walked away. As Riley Jackson loaded the last of his lovely wife's possessions into his best friend's Lear jet he expected at least an echo of that pain.

It didn't happen. The plane was now a sliver on the horizon and he felt no desolation at all.

Maybe he was cured of this love business. He obviously didn't have what it took to hold a relationship together and he no longer cared.

'What do you reckon, boy?' he asked his dog, and Bustle nosed his hand in gentle query. Bustle wouldn't miss Lisa either. Lisa had no time for dogs.

'We're on our own now, mate,' Riley told him as he turned to walk back to the house. The old dog limped beside him. Unlike his wife, Bustle would be loyal to the end.

Losing Bustle would be real heartache, Riley thought. That would be the real end of loving.

Bustle nosed his fingers again, and Riley stooped to give his ancient collie a gentle hug.

'I know. I don't have you for much longer, boy, and I'll miss you like crazy. But I'll miss nobody else. No one is going to get close to me, ever again.'

CHAPTER ONE

MISTAKE. Major mistake. On a mistake scale of one to ten, this ranked at about a thousand.

For as far as Jenna could see there was red dust and railway track. A few low-growing saltbushes grew along the line. In the distance, the train was fading into shimmering heat.

There was nothing else.

Jenna stood motionless, trying to take in the enormity of what she'd done.

When the announcement had been made that the train would stop at Barinya Downs, Jenna had assumed it was some sort of town. She'd glanced out the window and half a dozen trucks had been pulled up at the platform. Staff from the train had been unloading goods, and wide-hatted, farming-type men and women had been tossing the unloaded goods into the backs of their trucks.

It had to be a settlement at least, she'd decided, which was infinitely preferable to two more days on the train watching Brian humiliate his little daughter.

But she hadn't checked. She'd been so angry that she'd hurled their suitcases from the train and told Karli they were getting off. They'd stepped out onto the platform just as the train had started to move.

So where were they?

Barinya Downs.

The name meant nothing.

Worse. The trucks she'd seen a few minutes ago had now disappeared in a cloud of red dust.

There was nothing here at all.

She stared about her in horror, taking in her surroundings with sickening disbelief. What had she done? Where had she landed them? They were a day and a half's train journey from Sydney and two days from Perth.

They were nowhere.

'Where are we?' Karli asked, in the scared little voice that was all she ever used within Brian's hearing. It was the only tone Jenna had heard for the last two days.

'We're at Barinya Downs,' she said, speaking loudly into the hot wind, as if naming the place with gusto would give it substance.

It didn't. Barinya Downs seemed to consist of a concrete platform and a tin roof. That was it. There wasn't a tree. There wasn't a telephone. Nothing.

And Karli was standing by her side, waiting for her to tell her what to do.

Good grief, Jenna, you've really done it now, she whispered to herself. You king-sized twit. Dad always said you were stupid and he's been proved right.

But what her father thought no longer mattered. Charles Svenson was in America.

Maybe her father was even acting in collusion with Brian.

The thought was unbelievable, but it was certainly possible. She and Karli shared a mother, but their different fathers—Brian and Charles—had to be the most unscrupulous men she knew.

So Charles was no help, and Brian was on the train that was drawing further away by the minute.

Jenna closed her eyes, remembering Brian's face as she'd prepared to alight.

'Get off, then,' he snarled. 'See if I care. I've won.' His expression as she and her little half-sister stepped off the train was pure triumph.

Had he realised what this place was? Jenna's breath caught in horror as the thought struck home. Had Brian realised what she was doing? Had he known that Barinya Downs was nothing?

Surely even Brian wouldn't wish his daughter to be so desperately stranded.

Surely nothing. She sat down on her suitcase and tried to fight panic. She'd been so stupid. Five-year-old Karli was looking at her in concern, and she tugged the little girl down onto her knee and hugged her hard.

Calm down, she told herself. Make yourself think.

'Will someone come and get us?' Karli asked, her tone totally trusting, and Jenna struggled to find an answer.

'Maybe,' she told her. 'I need to figure things out.'

Karli obediently subsided into silence—a feat she was all too good at. Karli had spent her whole five and three-quarter years being seen and not heard. Jenna was determined her silence had to end, but for now she was grateful for Karli's silence. She had to think what to do.

Which was hard.

As well as being panic-stricken, Jenna was almost unbearably hot. They'd emerged from an air-conditioned train into an outside world so scorching it could almost bake bread. It was the middle of the day in the Australian Outback.

Forget the heat. Think, she told herself.

When would the next train come through?

She forced herself to remember the timetable she'd studied back in England. Brian's suggestion that they take the long train journey across the centre of Australia had been a surprise, and she'd looked the train's route and timetable up on the internet.

Think, she told herself desperately once more. I must be wrong.

She wasn't. She was sure she wasn't. The train ran across the continent only twice a week. As well as unloading goods, the stop at Barinya Downs had been to allow the train running in the opposite direction to pass them. It had rumbled through ten minutes ago.

There'd be no more trains for three days, she thought. This was Thursday. There was no train until next Monday.

Feeling sicker by the minute, Jenna hauled her cell phone from her bag and stared at the screen.

No host.

She was out of range of any of the communication carriers. Of course. What did she expect?

But she'd seen those guys in the trucks. They have to live somewhere, she told herself. She put Karli gently aside and walked to the edge of the platform. That was another mistake. The force of the midday sun hit her like a blast from a furnace.

She recoiled into the shade, and Karli snuggled back against her, finding security in the curves of her body.

Great security she was.

'We'll be fine, Karli,' she whispered. She narrowed her eyes against the glare, gazing around in a three-sixty-degree sweep. Surely somewhere there had to be something.

There were rough tracks leading in half a dozen directions from the siding. Nothing else.

No. Something.

There was definitely something, she thought as she came to the end of her sweep. Buildings? She wasn't sure. It was too far to see.

She stared down at her half-sister in indecision. What to do?

There was little choice. They could stay on this platform with nothing to eat, and—worse—nothing to drink, and wait for the next train. That was the stuff of nightmares. Or they could walk to whatever it was on the horizon.

She thought back to literature she'd read when they were preparing for this trip. 'In the case of breakdown in the Outback stay with your car,' was the advice. 'Tell people where you're going. Your friends will send out a search party and they'll find a car. They may well not find someone wandering in the desert.'

That was fine as far as advice went, she thought bitterly. But the only person who knew they were stuck here was Brian.

The vision of Brian's face floated before her. She'd never seen such malice.

He'd do nothing. They'd walked into his con brilliantly. She knew he'd do nothing and the thought made her feel ill.

How could she ever have trusted him?

Let it go, she told herself. Don't even think about it. We're going to have to look after ourselves.

So what was new?

We need to wait, she told herself. She glanced at her watch. One o'clock. The heat was at its peak. 'We'll change into something sensible,' she told Karli. 'Then in a few hours we can head over and see whether that's a house. If it's not we can always come back. We can always…'

Always what?

Good question.

'What will we do while we wait?' Karli asked.

That was another good question. They had to do something. The alternative was thinking and who wanted to think?

'We could make dust-castles,' she suggested, and Karli looked doubtful.

'You don't make dust-castles. You make sand-castles.'

'Yes, but that's according to the rules,' Jenna told her and she finally managed a smile. 'We're in unchartered territory now, sweetheart, and rules need to be stood on their head. Dust-castles it is.'

Riley walked in the back door and dumped the last of the supplies on the kitchen floor. Then he stood back and stared down in distaste. He'd hoped to be out of here by now, and even though the supplies Maggie had sent were necessary he didn't have to like them.

Baked beans. More baked beans.

Beer.

Another week, he told himself, and then he'd be back in civilisation. Back to Munyering, with his lovely house, Maggie's great food and a swimming pool. All the things that made life in this heat bearable.

Why hadn't he sent one of his men to do this job?

Because they wouldn't come, he told himself, and he even managed a wry grin. There was bound to be something in the union rules about existing on baked beans and dust.

But he was wasting time, talking to himself in this dump of a kitchen, and time was something he didn't have. So... Priorities.

He unloaded the beer into the fridge, packing it in until the door barely shut.

'That's my housekeeping,' he told himself and then he gave another rueful grin. Damn, wasn't talking to himself the first sign of madness? Maybe he should get another dog.

Maybe he shouldn't.

It was just after one o'clock. He had seven hours of daylight left. That was at least one more bore that could be mended.

What do they say about mad dogs and Englishmen? he demanded of himself, but he already knew the answer. Working in the midday sun might well lead to madness, but the bores were blocked and the survival of his cattle depended on him getting them unblocked. If he rested, maybe another thirty head of stock would be dead before nightfall.

'Okay, mate,' he told himself, looking at the beer with real longing. 'That'll wait. It has to. Get yourself back to work.'

* * *

As sunsets went this one was amazing. The sun was a ball of fire low on the horizon, and the blaze of light across the desert would, in normal circumstances, have taken Jenna's breath away.

Not now. Karli was starting to stumble. The buildings had looked a mile or so away when she'd judged distance from the railway siding, but it'd ended up being closer to three or four miles. They'd abandoned their luggage back at the siding and were wearing only light pants, shirts and casual shoes, but even then it had been a long, hot walk. The sand was burning and their shoes were far too thin.

And now… The closer they grew to the buildings, the more Jenna's heart sank.

The homestead looked abandoned. It consisted of ancient, unpainted weatherboards, and its rusty iron roof looked none too weatherproof. There were no fences or marked garden—just more red dust. All around the house were tumbledown sheds. The house itself looked intact, but only just. Broken windows and missing weatherboards told Jenna that no one had been at home here for a long time.

But it was no longer the house that interested Jenna. No matter how ramshackle it was, it could be a shelter until the next train came through. What she'd focussed on for the last half-mile was the water tank behind the house. It looked as if it might tumble down at any minute, but it still looked workable.

'Please,' she was whispering as she led Karli past the first of the shacks. 'Please…'

And then she stopped dead.

Behind the house, at the end of a crude airstrip, was an aeroplane. Small. Expensive. New.

It wasn't the sort of plane anyone in their right mind would abandon.

'There must be someone here,' Jenna told Karli, and she crouched in the dust and gave her little half-sister a hug. 'Oh, well done. You've walked really bravely, and now we're safe. Someone's here.'

'I need a drink,' Karli said cautiously and Jenna collected herself. A drink.

She turned and stared at the house, willing someone to appear. No one did.

'Let's knock,' she told Karli.

Who'd live in a dump like this?

She led her sister over to the house and she felt about as old as Karli was—and maybe even more scared.

She knocked.

No one answered.

They waited. Karli stood trustingly by Jenna's side and Jenna's sense of responsibility grew by the minute.

Come on. Answer.

Nothing. The only sound was the wind, blasting around the corners of the house.

'Knock again,' Karli whispered, and Jenna tried again, louder.

The door sagged inward.

A couple of loose sheets of roofing iron crashed down and down again in the wind.

Nothing.

'I'm really thirsty,' Karli told her, and Jenna's grip on her hand tightened. This wasn't London. Surely anyone who lived here would understand their need to break in. And...they didn't need to break. The door was falling in anyway.

'Let's go inside,' she whispered.

'Why are we whispering?' Karli asked.

'Because it's creepy. Hold my hand tight.'

'You think there might be ghosts?'

'If there are, I hope they can fly aeroplanes.'

Karli giggled. It was a great sound. There hadn't been enough giggling in Karli's short life, Jenna thought. There'd been none at all on the train with her father, and for the first time Jenna decided that maybe it hadn't been such a disaster to get off.

If there was water. If the pilot of the aeroplane wasn't an axe murderer.

Axe murderer? She was going nuts here. She didn't have time to indulge in axe-murderer fantasies.

No one was going to answer the door.

She adjusted her grip on Karli's hand to very, very tight. For Karli, Jenna told herself hastily. To reassure Karli. Not to reassure herself.

They tiptoed inside.

Through the back door the place looked much like the outside—as if it had been deserted for years. There was thick dust coating every surface. But...there were footprints in the dust. The prints looked as if they were made by a man's boots, and they seemed relatively fresh.

Holding Karli's hand as if it were infinitely important that she didn't let go, Jenna led her across the bare wooden floorboards of the entrance porch. Their shoes left much smaller footprints beside the big ones.

The next door led to the kitchen.

Here there were definitely signs of life. There were boxes of canned food, a kerosene fridge, a lamp and a pile of newspapers strewn over a big wooden table. While Karli gazed around her with interest Jenna picked up the top newspaper. It was dated two days ago.

Someone was definitely using the house.

And—even better—there was a sink. Above the sink was a tap. Hardly daring to breathe, Jenna released Karli's hand and twisted the tap. Out ran a stream of pure, clear water. She lowered her head and drank and nothing had ever tasted so good.

'We're fine, Karli,' she said, a trifle unsteadily, and she lifted the little girl so that she, too, could drink. 'We're safe. There's food and there's drink. We can stay here for as long as we need.'

'The hell you can.'

She twisted, still holding Karli to the tap. There was a man in the doorway.

For a moment there was absolute silence. Karli was still drinking and Jenna was shocked past speaking.

The man was large. He was well over six feet tall, and he filled the doorway with his broad shoulders and his strongly muscled frame. His build indicated a life of hard, physical work.

So did the rest of him. The man's hair was sun-bleached, from dark brown at the roots to almost gold at the tips, and his skin was a deep lined bronze. The harsh contours of his strongly boned face were softened by deep, grey eyes that creased at the corners, maybe in accustomed defence against the sun's glare. The man's clothes—his hands, his face—were ingrained by layer upon layer of dust.

He had to be a farmer. The man's whole appearance labelled him as such. He wore moleskin trousers and a khaki shirt, and in his hand he held a wide Akubra hat. This was an outfit Jenna recognised as almost a uniform among Australian men who worked the land.

Was he a farmer here? It didn't make sense.

She had to speak. She had to say something.

'H…hi.' Not so good. Her voice came out as a squeak, and the man's eyes widened.

'Hi, yourself.' Unlike Jenna's, the man's voice was deep, resonant and sure, laced with a broad Australian accent. His eyes were calmly watchful, as if at any minute he expected the apparition in his kitchen to vanish.

Jenna was still holding Karli to the tap. Now Karli finished drinking and pulled away. She lowered her to the ground; Karli stared distrustfully up at the stranger and then shrank against Jenna's leg.

'I… Is this your house?' Jenna managed, holding tight to Karli.

'It's my house.' The man was staring down at Karli as if he was certain he was seeing things.

Karli didn't look at him. She shrank behind Jenna's legs and stayed there.

Silence. For the life of her, Jenna couldn't think of what else to say.

Eventually, apparently recovering from the shock of finding strangers in his kitchen, the big man tossed his Akubra onto the table and walked across to the fridge. He opened the door and snagged a beer. Raising his eyebrows quizzically—for heaven's sake, was the guy laughing?—he lifted the can towards Jenna. 'I don't know who on earth you are or how you got here,' he said, 'but can I offer you a beer?'

'N…no. Thank you.'

'There's not much else,' the man told her, pulling the ring from the top of the can and taking a long, long swallow. He didn't lower the can until he'd almost emptied it. 'Apart from water,' he added then. 'Which you seem to have found all by yourselves.'

Karli ventured a peek at him then from behind Jenna's legs. Amazingly he gave the little girl a wink—which had her ducking back behind her sister.

'We did find your water.' Jenna took a deep breath, searching for composure. She didn't find it.

'I'm sorry. I guess…the thing is that we seem to be in a bit of trouble.'

'You know, I guessed that,' the man agreed gravely. 'Either that or you're a pair of very enthusiastic encyclopaedia salesmen.' The man smiled at her across his beer, and when he smiled it was all Jenna could do not to gasp. The smile lit his whole face, making him seem years younger. She'd guessed his age at somewhere around forty, but when he smiled she knew he was closer to thirty. And, as well as younger, his smile made him seem incredibly…incredibly…

Male. Gorgeous. Sexy. The adjectives suddenly crowded into her head, and instinctively her hands fell to hold Karli tighter.

She gave herself a sharp mental swipe. She was being ridiculous. She didn't react to men like this. She didn't.

So why was this man so…mesmeric?

'We're not salesmen,' she managed, striving for lightness. 'The doors are a bit far apart out here to do door-to-door selling.'

She had her reward. The laughter deepened behind his eyes at her pathetic attempt at humour.

'That's a pity,' he told her, his smile staying right where it was. He motioned to the pile of newspapers. 'This is about all I have in the way of reading matter. An encyclopaedia would have its uses.' Then his smile faded as he searched her eyes. The expression on his face softened, as though he sensed her fear. His gaze dropped again to Karli, peeping out from behind Jenna's legs, and his expression softened still further.

'So if you're not salesmen, maybe you could tell me who you are?'

'I don't think…' Jenna paused, the enormity of trying to explain their situation to this man almost overwhelming her in its degree of difficulty. 'You won't believe…'

'Try me.'

'But I don't even know who you are,' she burst out, and his gorgeous smile came flooding back.

'No,' he agreed. 'You don't. You know, I figured since you're in my kitchen and you came in uninvited, that maybe it was up to you to introduce yourselves first. But maybe I've been remiss.' He hauled his hat from the table and shoved it back on his head, then raised it a few inches in a gesture of salutation. 'I'm Riley Jackson.' His dark eyes twinkled down at Karli, who was still clinging as hard as she could cling to Jenna's leg. 'Have a seat, ladies. Make yourselves at home.'

Then he readdressed his beer. Duty done.

Jenna stared at him in confusion. She was way out of her depth, she acknowledged. If it weren't for Karli she'd walk out of here—take her chances on the railway platform.

Who was she kidding? No, she wouldn't. She had no choice but to keep on talking.

'I'm Jenna Svenson,' she told him. 'This is Karli.'

'I'm very pleased to meet you, Jenna and Karli,' he said gravely. 'Welcome to my farm.'

His farm. She stared around her at the layer upon layer of dust. She turned to stare out the cracked and grimed window at the dusty paddocks beyond. 'This isn't a working farm?' she managed. 'Surely. I mean…you don't live here?'

'Don't you like my décor?' Riley demanded, as if he were wounded to the core, and she blinked. 'What's wrong with it?'

'It's really dusty,' Karli volunteered and that shocked Jenna, too. For Karli to speak in the presence of a stranger was amazing. 'You don't wash your table,' the little girl said, and there was even a note of reproof in her tone.

'Hey, I would have dusted if I'd known you were coming.' Riley smiled straight down at the little girl, with what was almost a conspiratorial grin. 'I would have got out the best china and made a cake.

Or put some more beer in the fridge. Speaking of which.' He hauled open the fridge to snag another beer and Jenna bit her lip at the sight of it. Her fears had started to recede, but now they resurfaced with a vengeance. They were so alone. He might not be an axe murderer, but if he were to get drunk...

He saw her look. He stood with his hand on the refrigerator door and his eyebrows rose in a query. 'Does this worry you?' He raised his beer can.

'I...no.'

'It shouldn't,' he told her, and went straight to the heart of her fear. 'It's low-alcohol beer. I'd have to drink a bathful to get tight. And, lady, even if I was drinking full-strength beer, I've been working in the sun for the past twelve hours and after effort like that, alcohol hardly hits the sides.' His eyes narrowed. 'You sound English. Are you?'

'Y...yes.'

'Australian girls don't start getting nervous until their men down a dozen or more.' He pulled the ring on his new can and took a long drink. 'Now, having reassured you that I'm not about to get rolling drunk on my second light beer, I figure it's your turn. Maybe I'm being picky but I would like to know what the hell—' his eyes fell to Karli and he corrected himself '—what on earth you guys are doing in my kitchen, criticising my housekeeping and counting my beers. It's not that I'm unappreciative. It's always nice when guests drop in. I'm just not sure where you dropped from.'

She swallowed. He had the right. 'From the train,' she started and he nodded.

'I guess it had to be the train. But I was over there picking up supplies. I didn't see you.'

'We got off just as the train left.'

'You weren't expecting to be collected, then?'

'No.'

'I see.' He thought about it, his eyes not leaving hers. 'So you thought you might indulge in a little sightseeing?'

'There's no need to be sarcastic,' Jenna snapped. 'We didn't choose to get off.'

'You're saying someone threw you off?' That amazing smile flashed out then. 'What, for being drunk and disorderly?' As she didn't reply, he settled onto a chair with the air of a man about to enjoy a good book. 'Well, well. Jenna Svenson. And Karli. Sit down and tell me all. Please.'

She owed him that much, she thought. She needed him. She had to tell him.

She sat and hoisted Karli onto the chair beside her. Their chairs were touching and Karli was still in contact with her, but strangely the little girl seemed to be relaxing.

What was it about this man?

Jenna wasn't relaxing. She sat gingerly on the edge of her chair. The chair gave a distinct wobble, and the wobble made her feel even more precarious. It was as if her world were tilting and she wasn't at all sure that she wasn't about to slide right off.

'We had a disagreement with someone on the train,' she managed. 'We...we got angry and we got off.'

'You had a disagreement.' His thoughtful eyes glinted again, humour seemingly just below the surface. His eyes searched her face, then dropped to take her all in. His eyes ran over her dust-stained pants and blouse—they'd once been white—over her wind-tumbled curls where the red dust was blending with her burnt-red hair, down to her slim arms resting on the table before her. To her bare fingers.

His eyes went again to Karli. To study her dusty red curls and her big green eyes that were a mirror image of Jenna's.

'Who was your disagreement with?'

'With Karli's father,' she told him. 'Brian.'

His eyes flashed again to her fingers but there was no ring-mark there. That was what he was searching for, she knew. Damn him, she thought with anger. She knew exactly what he was thinking.

'Oh, dear,' he said. 'You've left the third part of your happy family on the train.'

'There's no third part,' she snapped. 'And, believe me, it's no happy family.'

'Obviously.'

She flushed. She opened her mouth to say something, but nothing came out. How to explain within Karli's earshot?

And how to justify her stupidity? Her stupid, almost criminal idiocy.

'You know, what you did wasn't all that bright,' he told her, his voice gentle and his eyes resting thoughtfully on her flushed face.

'I know that. But when I looked out there were people on the platform. It looked like a busy little country siding. I thought there'd be somewhere where we could stay until the next train came through. It wasn't until we got off and everyone had disappeared that I remembered trains only come through twice a week.'

'You did that with a child?' he said, and there was suddenly a flash of anger behind the gentleness. She bit her lip. Okay, he was angry and

maybe she deserved that. She was angry with herself. But if he'd seen the way Brian had treated
Karli—the way she'd cringed....

'I had my reasons,' she said, in a tight little voice
in which weariness was starting to show. 'Believe
me. I was dumb but I had no choice.' She hesitated.
This wasn't easy. To ask a complete stranger for
such a favour... 'But you have a plane,' she said.
'We saw it when we came round the side of the
house. We...' She hesitated because the blaze of
anger was still there, but she had to ask. 'Could...is
it possible that you'd fly us out?' Then, as the anger
deepened she went on fast. 'I'd pay you, of course.'
Somehow she'd pay. 'I'm not asking favours.'
When had she ever asked a favour of anyone?

He gazed at her, his eyes expressionless. 'You
want me to drop everything and fly you out of here.
To where?'

'Adelaide?'

'Adelaide?' he demanded, incredulous.

'Please.' Her hold on Karli tightened. Dear
heaven, she'd got them in such a mess. She'd believed Brian. Why on earth had she ever believed
Brian?

She'd wanted to believe him. For Karli's sake.

'I don't know what to do,' she confessed. 'We
can't stay here.'

'No,' he agreed. 'You can't.'

'If not Adelaide...' she shrugged '...just any-where with a hotel and a telephone and some way of getting back to the outside world.'

'No.'

'No?'

'The nearest place with those sort of facilities is Adelaide,' he said flatly. 'That's several hours' flight in my small plane. It'd take me a day to get you there and get back here, and I don't have a day free. I'm sorry to be disobliging, but I'm on a dead-line.'

'A deadline?' She stared around in incredulity. 'What sort of deadline can you have in a place like this?'

Riley's expression became absolutely still. 'Careful,' he said softly. 'Not so much of the dis-dain, if you please. This is my farm we're talking of.'

'But...' Jenna closed her eyes for a fraction of a moment, to give herself space. She'd never felt so foreign or alone or out of control in her life—and she'd been alone for ever.

'I'm sorry,' she managed, and she fought for the courage to open her eyes again and face him. 'I guess... Look, I don't understand Australian farms. This is the first one I've been on. For all I know—' she searched desperately for a smile '—this could be luxury accommodation.'

'It isn't,' he said flatly. 'But I have a roof over my head and a refrigerator full of beer. What more could I want?'

Anything, she thought. Anything.

'The other people at the siding,' she asked. 'I don't suppose…if they're on farms, would one of them be able to fly us out?'

'Those other farms are half a day's drive to get to,' he told her. 'My nearest neighbour is over a hundred miles north over rough, unmade tracks. They came to the siding to get supplies from the train and they probably won't be back at the siding for another couple of weeks. Today was the main supply run.'

Dear God.

'We're stuck here,' she whispered.

'Unless I kick you out, yes.'

Karli looked up at Riley then, with what, for the child, was an almost superhuman amount of courage. 'Will you make us go back and sit on the train platform by ourselves until the next train comes?' she whispered.

Jenna opened her mouth, and then thought better of it. Shut up, she told herself. Just shut up. She couldn't ask that question any better than Karli just had.

Riley was staring at them with exasperation. 'Your mother's a dope,' Riley told the little girl.

It was the wrong thing to say. Jenna flinched, and within her arms she felt Karli flinch as well.

'My mother's dead,' Karli whispered. 'She died yesterday.'

CHAPTER TWO

THERE was no way of softening the awfulness.

Riley knew Karli was speaking the truth. Jenna watched his face, knowing that he'd heard the shock and the raw pain in Karli's voice.

He'd heard the despair of abandonment.

'I'm sorry,' Riley said at last. He set his beer on the table—very carefully, as if it might break. He looked from Karli to Jenna and back again. 'I assumed you two were mother and daughter.' He compressed his mouth and focussed on Karli. 'Who's this lady, then?'

'Jenna's my big sister,' Karli whispered. 'Sort of.'

'Sort of?'

'We're half-sisters,' Jenna told him. 'Nicole, our mother—we're the product of two of her marriages.'

'Two—?'

'Look, this isn't getting anything sorted,' Jenna said, and she was starting to sound as desperate as she felt. Karli was wilting against her. The shock and horror of the last few hours were taking their toll and it was amazing the little girl was still upright. She pulled her up to sit on her lap. 'So you can't take us anywhere?'

He hesitated, but then he shook his head. 'No,' he told her and there was even regret in his voice. 'I'm sorry, but my labour's not for sale. I have blocked bores and my cattle are dying because they can't get anything to drink. If I leave before the bores are operational then I'll lose cattle by the hundred, and their deaths won't be pretty. I'm not being disobliging for the sake of it. I have urgent priorities.'

She bit her lip. 'I'm sorry.' This was getting harder by the minute. He was a man in a hurry and the last thing he needed was to be saddled with a woman and a child. 'I was really stupid to get off the train.'

'You were.'

'But it's done now,' she said with a flash of anger. She sounded like a wimp, she decided, and a wimp was the last way she'd have described herself. She'd been looking after herself since she was knee-high to a grasshopper. It was men who'd got her into this mess and this guy was of the same species.

'Can you at least put us up here until the next train comes through?' Then, at the look on his face, she went on in a hurry. 'Please. We'll be no trouble.' She had to persuade him. What choice did she have?

What choice did he have?

'I don't have any choice,' he muttered, echoing her own thoughts. Then he looked again at Karli and he relented. He even smiled again. 'It's a pretty funny place to stay and I bet it's not what you're used to, but you're very welcome.'

He smiled across at Karli, and the child stared at him for a long moment and then tried to smile back.

'You're nice,' she whispered. She nestled closer to Jenna. 'He's nicer than my daddy.'

'Yeah, well, that'd be hard,' Jenna said with some asperity, but she fondled the little girl's curls and looked across at Riley.

'Thank you,' she said. 'If there's really no choice…'

'You know, we could always contact the flying doctor and ask them to collect you,' he said, suddenly helpful. 'We could say you were psychiatrically unhinged.'

'Gee, thanks.'

'It might work. They have a psychiatric service.'

'You're being very helpful!'

'Well, I think I am,' he told her, but his eyes were still resting on Karli with concern. He was making light of it for Karli's sake, she realised. 'I've let you drink my water and sit at my kitchen table and if you decide to take up my very generous offer of accommodation I'll even let you share my baked beans. Then I'll offer you both a spare bed and keep you fed and watered until the next train comes through.' He hesitated. 'You realise just how much danger you put yourselves in? This man you were with. Brian. Will he realise and send a search party?'

'No,' Jenna said flatly. 'He won't.'

'You don't want to contact the police?'

That was a thought. But…contact the police and say what? That they'd been conned? She could get a message to her father, but she wasn't at all sure that her father wasn't in cahoots with Brian. There was no guarantee that he'd help.

They were two like pieces of low-life. Her father and Jenna's father.

And their mother was dead.

'We're on our own,' she said, with what she hoped was an attempt at cheerfulness. 'Just Karli and me. But if you could put us up we'd be very, very appreciative.'

'As opposed to very, very dead if I threw you out into the heat.'

'Like your cattle,' she agreed bluntly. 'Yes. We'll try not to be any trouble.'

'I can't afford you to be any trouble,' he told her. He pushed back his chair and rose. The decision had been made and he obviously needed to move on. 'If you'll excuse me,' he told her. 'I'm hot and filthy and exhausted and I'm having difficulty making my head work. I need to dip myself under cold water before I play host.'

Once more he smiled down at Karli. His smile was warm and strong and caring—but it didn't include Jenna.

'We'll discuss food and beds when I'm clean,' he told her. 'But I'm carrying too much dust to be sociable. Don't go away. Or if you do, make sure you fill a few water bottles first. It's a good four days' walk to my nearest neighbour and as far as I know no one's ever walked it. No one would be mad enough to try.'

And he walked out of the kitchen and left Jenna to her confusion.

The first thing she needed to concentrate on was Karli. The little girl's eyes were closing and her body was slumping.

Jenna thought again of Brian and her anger rose to almost overwhelm her.

Damn him, damn him, damn him, she muttered to herself. Damn them. Because suddenly it was a group. Jenna's father. Her father. Her mother. And Riley was there too. All rolled up into one ball of fury.

Which was illogical, she told herself. Riley wasn't to blame. He was stuck.

He had a lovely, gleaming aeroplane that could transport her to a comfortable hotel somewhere near an airport and...

And his cattle would die. She had no doubt he was telling the truth. He looked exhausted. He looked like a man who was working far harder than a man should. The way he'd left to have a shower seemed almost an act of desperation. It spoke of a man past the limits of exhaustion, trying to clear his head and see things straight.

No. She couldn't blame him.

And the rest?

Her mother was dead.

She thought of Nicole, and tried to dredge up a feeling of sadness, but all she felt was bitterness. Bitterness at how she herself had been treated, but, worse, bitterness at what had happened to Karli.

Nicole was dead. Of course. It wasn't the least surprising. What was surprising was that, leading the life she had, their mother had survived so long.

It's all about surviving, she told herself drearily. That was what she had to do now. Survive.

Karli's eyes were now completely closed. Jenna rose, carrying her with her. At almost six years old, Karli should be too big to lift, but the child was seriously underweight. She carried her across to the cracked window and gazed out into the fading light. The land was disappearing into the dusk, but she could still make out the horizon—long and endlessly flat.

There was nothing here. Where were these cattle Riley talked about? Figments of his imagination? What on earth was the man doing, working a useless, barren piece of land?

Surely he can't make a living off this place, she thought, but then she thought of his aeroplane and her confusion grew. The plane was obviously expensive. How could this farm generate enough income to provide such a thing?

'Well, at least he's not a drug baron growing cash crops of opium,' she told the sleeping Karli. 'There's hardly a lush crop of poppies in this backyard. If he's making money from this place he must have found a market for bottled dust.'

She turned back to the kitchen. It was littered with crates and cardboard boxes, with everything covered in dust. There was a small gas stove and a kerosene fridge and little else. Ugh.

What of the rest of the house? She hadn't been invited to look—but she couldn't keep holding Karli for ever. She had to find somewhere she could lay her down.

The kitchen door led to a sitting room—of sorts. It held a few chairs and an old settee. In the corner was an ancient gramophone. But one of the window-panes was smashed, and dust was everywhere.

What next? There were two rooms leading off the sitting room. Jenna pushed the doors wide and reacted again with horror. These must be the bedrooms. Iron bedsteads stood as islands in the dust, with lumpy mattresses on sagging springs. Both rooms had broken windows, and once again they were thick with dust.

Surely Riley didn't sleep here? Neither room looked as if it had seen a human for years. She retreated in haste, Karli growing heavier by the minute.

Riley must sleep somewhere. Where was he now?

She returned to the sitting room and stared out. Beyond the filthy windows was a veranda, and a door opened out to it. This must be the formal front door.

Did anyone ever come here?

She shoved the door open and walked outside, wary of broken floorboards, but there was no need for caution. In the lee of the house, the veranda was out of the wind and thus protected from the all-pervading dust.

In the fading light, Jenna could see a big bed at each end of the veranda, one made up with sheets and what looked like comfortable pillows. This, then, must be where Riley slept.

Riley's bed or not, it was the most inviting place in the house. She laid Karli down with care, and watched as the little girl snuggled contentedly into the pillows. Karli had no cares to stop her sleeping. Jenna would take care of her.

Would she? Could she?

What had she got them both into?

This was such a mess, she thought ruefully. How had it happened? Jenna had taken such care to be independent, but Karli had been catapulted into her life with a vengeance, and how could she walk away?

She ran a finger down Karli's dust-stained face, aching with tenderness for a child she was starting to love in a way she'd never thought possible. Where to go from here? How could she cope with this situation? With Riley Jackson? With her future?

One step at a time, she thought. Just live in the moment, otherwise you'll go mad.

She turned and stared at the other bed at the far end of the veranda. It had a mattress and a couple of pillows. It looked almost comfortable.

It was too close to Riley's bed.

The alternative was the railway siding, she told herself, and grimaced. It wasn't an alternative at all. But to share sleeping quarters with that man…

The door opened at the end of the veranda—and that man was right in front of her.

Naked.

He'd obviously just emerged from the shower. His hair was still dripping. His towel was draped over his shoulder—but it wasn't covering what needed to be covered.

She was a nurse, she told herself desperately. She was used to naked men.

She wasn't used to this one.

There was no mistaking the magnificence of Riley's body. He was built like a Rodin sculpture, she decided as she bit back an exclamation of dismay and moved swiftly to block the line of sight between Riley and the sleeping child. Then, with her complexion fast changing colour, she made herself look at his face—which was a better place to focus on than where her eyes were automatically drawn.

Her colour deepened further. The man was laughing!

'Whoops,' he said as he slung his towel around his waist to make himself respectable. Almost respectable. 'I'm not used to visitors. Um…welcome to my bedroom.'

Which made Jenna's flushing face turn to beetroot. She was in his bedroom. What else did she expect?

'I…I'm sorry,' she muttered. She motioned back to Karli who was thankfully still soundly asleep. 'I needed… She needed…'

He followed her gaze and his face softened with understanding. 'Of course. I'm sorry. I should have thought of that before I showered.'

'I'll move her.'

'There's no need.' He snagged his clothes from the bedside chair, then caught his towel as it started to slip. 'I'll dress in the wash house. Meet you in the kitchen in five minutes.'

He disappeared and she had a fleeting thought that suddenly he was as discomposed as she was.

Was that possible?

*   *   *

Five minutes later when they met again back in the kitchen, her colour still hadn't subsided. The gathering dusk helped, but then Riley produced a kerosene lantern and turned the little kitchen's darkness to light. Her colour rose all over again.

He was respectable now, but only just. He was wearing faded jeans and nothing else. When he'd been covered in grimed clothes and dust, Jenna had thought the man was seriously good-looking, but now he was naked from the waist up, his broad chest was tanned and rippled, and his strongly boned face was rid of its dusty coating. The whole package meant Jenna had to fight not to gasp.

That and the memory of what she'd just seen…

She wasn't interested in men, she told herself desperately. She'd never been interested in men. She'd seen what so-called romance did to women's lives and she wanted no part of it. She'd been independent for ever and she intended to stay that way.

But the sight of Riley…

You can appreciate a good body without wanting it, she told herself fiercely, but still her face burned. She was way out of her comfort zone here. She was half a world out of her comfort zone.

Where was a magic carpet when she needed one?

'I'm sorry we went into your bedroom,' she managed and he smiled, a gentle, quizzical smile that was strangely at odds with the image she had of him as a man's man. A threatening specimen of the male species. His smile was almost tender.

'You hadn't thought I might come out starkers.' He took in her burning colour and grinned. 'My apologies. I'm not used to women in my house. I'll see that I stay respectable in the future.'

In future. Help. Jenna's breath caught in panic as she stared across at this large, disconcerting male. She was stuck here for three days.

'Can I interest you in baked beans?'

It was a thoughtful drawl from Riley and she looked up at his face, sharply suspicious. It was as if he could read her thoughts. She didn't like the sensation.

Food. Concentrate on food. In truth, she must be hungry. She hadn't eaten since breakfast. She needed to wake Karli and persuade her to eat as well. But baked beans? Karli hardly ate anything and to persuade her to eat beans seemed impossible.

Once more her thoughts must have shown on her face, because Riley's dark eyes creased into laughter.

'This place is not a five-star restaurant, lady,' he told her.

'No.' Trying to get her face in order, she knelt by the crate that seemed to hold all the food cans. 'Do you have nothing but beans? You'll get scurvy.'

'Yeah, but I'll die happy.' He was standing above her, disconcertingly male. Disconcertingly big. 'I like beans.'

'I don't.'

'Lady…'

'And neither does Karli,' she said, unconscious of the fact that he was staring down at her with a very strange expression on his face. 'I need to make her eat. Surely you don't just exist on baked beans. No one could.'

'I'm tough.'

'Yeah, but surely not stupid. Or not that stupid.' She was lifting cans out and inspecting their labels. Spaghetti. Baked beans. Spaghetti. Baked beans. But at the bottom were a few different labels, tossed in as if the packer hadn't expected them to be used but had put them in as if to satisfy a conscience. They were cans of interesting things like water chestnuts, snow peas and capsicum. There were a few packets of herbs and spices. A few withered onions lay ignored underneath, and there was also a large packet of rice.

'Can I use these?' she asked, and Riley stooped beside her to take a look. His bare chest brushed her arm. He was so close. She edged away and almost toppled over. His hand came out and steadied her—which didn't steady her in the least.

'I opened a can of those water chestnut things once,' he told her as if he was totally unaware of how aware of his closeness she was. 'I tipped them over spaghetti. They tasted like—'

'I can imagine how they tasted,' Jenna said faintly. 'Why did you pack them if you don't like them?'

'I didn't pack them. Maggie packs for me. I make her put in the beans and spaghetti, but she always shoves in a few of those foreign jobs.' He grinned and held up his hands as if in surrender. 'You and Maggie would get along fine. You have a common interest in scurvy. Maggie says at the first sign of bandy legs or bleeding gums I'm to open them and eat them, regardless.'

'Sensible woman.' She sorted through the cans some more, still achingly aware of his body. 'So who's Maggie? Your wife?'

'A wife?' Was she imagining it or was there suddenly a trace of bitterness in his words. 'No, ma'am. Maggie is…well, Maggie is my resident scurvy defence.'

'She's not resident here.'

'Very acute, Miss Svenson. No, Maggie is not here. This place was my woman-free zone until you and Karli arrived, and I hope it will be again very soon.'

'You don't like women, then?' It was a stupid question, she conceded. She had no business asking, but it just came out of left field. Then she had to concentrate on her cans as Riley stared at her and disconcerted her all over again.

There was a long silence. Finally he spoke again, and when he did Jenna knew she'd been right when she'd thought she detected bitterness. She'd hit a nerve and the nerve was still raw.

'It's not that I don't like women,' he told her. 'It's just that I don't have time for them.'

'Except for Maggie.'

'As you say.' He smiled at that. 'Yep. Hooray for Maggie.' He lifted a can of beans. 'Let's get these heated. I need to go to bed.'

'Let me cook,' she told him, rising with her hands full of the smaller cans. 'Give me ten minutes and I'll throw together something that's edible.'

'Beans are edible.' He sounded hurt.

'Not in my book,' she retorted. Then at the look on his face—for heaven's sake, he looked like a pup who'd just been kicked!—she relented. 'Tell you what. You try what I cook, and if you don't like it you can heat your beans. How's that for a deal?'

'Very generous—seeing it's my food.'

Jenna grinned. 'Noble's my middle name. Why don't you go away and I'll call you when it's ready?'

'What, sit in the parlour and watch television on my chaise longue?' Riley settled his long body onto a chair and placed his bare feet on the table. He leaned back, tilting his chair at a precarious angle and crossing his arms with the air of a man settling down to watch a show. 'No way, Miss Svenson. For one thing, televisions and chaises longues are thin on the ground around here. For another, if you're cooking my food then it's my job to supervise. I can see that it's my duty and I'm not a man to shirk my duty—especially if I can do it with a can of cold beer in my hand.'

'Fine, then.' Jenna swallowed the qualms she was feeling about being supervised by such a disconcerting male and she even managed a smile. She plonked two onions on the table, turned to the sink to collect a knife, and then faced him square on. 'There is just one decision to be made.'

'Which is?' Riley was watching her with sudden caution. Which might have something to do with the very large knife she was now holding.

'You have a choice,' she told him. 'The menu at the moment is stir-fried vegetables and rice, Chinese style. But unless those feet are removed, Riley Jackson, I'm adding fresh meat. Stir-fried toes, to be precise.'

She raised her knife.

There was a moment's startled silence. He stared at the knife. He stared at his toes.

He stared at her.

His face changed.

It was as if he thought she meant her threat, she thought incredulously. Or maybe…maybe she was threatening something else. Something he didn't want threatened.

The silence went on and on. Finally, still staring straight at her, he removed the offending toes.

'Sorry, ma'am,' he drawled and it was as if his drawl was to hide some deeper emotion. He sat back and steadied his chair. 'My toes aren't on anyone's menu.'

'Just as well,' she managed, lowering her knife and looking at the man before her with a slight frown. It was as if there were an electric charge underlying this light-hearted banter and she didn't understand it one bit. 'It's my bet any toes of yours would be as tough as old boots.'

CHAPTER THREE

IF THERE was one thing Jenna prided herself on, it was her ability to cook. Years of long school holidays where she'd been alone and a childhood where her only friends had been servants had driven her into the kitchen of her parents' various homes and hotels. There she'd met possibly the only kindness she knew. In the process she'd learned fabulous cooking.

She needed all her skills now. To make a decent stir-fry with two fresh(ish) onions and everything else from cans was a skill in itself.

'Why don't you just chuck the lot together and stir?' Riley demanded as she drained and dried every can of vegetables.

'Because I'd end up with stew.'

'What's wrong with stew?'

'To someone who survives on baked beans, probably nothing. But some of us have taste.'

He smiled, a low, lazy smile that had her curiously unsettled as he watched some more. 'Why are you putting those vegetables to one side?'

'I'll feed Karli the basics. Rice and sauce will be easy to feed her when she's three-quarters asleep. Then I'll reheat and stir the crunchy vegetables in just before you and I eat. There's nothing worse than snow peas that don't crunch.'

'I thought there was nothing worse than baked beans.'

'Baked beans don't even count in the worse stakes,' Jenna said darkly. 'Okay. Done. Stir this while I wake Karli.'

Somewhat to her surprise he did stir. Then, as she carried a dopey, half-asleep little girl back into the kitchen he surprised her further by holding out his arms to take her.

She hesitated. She wasn't accustomed to receiving help and she half expected Karli to shy away. But Karli settled on Riley's lap without a murmur, gazed at Jenna with eyes that were barely focussing and let herself be fed like a baby.

If she wasn't really hungry she wouldn't have been able to eat at all, Jenna thought, but she managed to get a good few mouthfuls into her before the little girl's eyes sank closed again.

'Thank you,' she whispered to Riley as she gathered Karli up again to take her back to bed.

'Think nothing of it.' He smiled again, and once again that strange, unsettled feeling swept over her.

She glanced at him uncertainly. But now wasn't the time to examine why he was making her feel as she was undoubtedly feeling. She had to focus on Karli.

It took her a few minutes to settle the little girl back into bed, and when she returned Riley was scooping the stir-fry onto two plates. He'd added the crunchy vegetables all on his own.

'I thought you'd never come,' he told her. 'I decided that your snow peas would definitely go soggy.'

'I thought you didn't care.'

'I care.' He gazed down to where every vegetable was clearly delineated in its succulent sauce, and the rice underneath was fluffy and fragrant. He closed his eyes and sniffed in appreciation. 'Believe me, I care.'

'What—with your baked beans going to waste in their crate?'

'I guess I could just try this to be nice,' he said grudgingly. He sat—and then had to make a wild grab for his plate as Jenna hauled it away. He missed. 'Hey!'

'There's no need to be polite on my account.' Jenna sat herself down with two plates before her. 'I'll nobly eat your share. You go bake your beans, Mr Jackson.'

His gorgeous grin swept back. 'Miss Svenson, can I have my dinner back?' His grin deepened as Jenna hauled his plate further away. 'I really would like to try your dinner—and it's greedy to eat that much by yourself.'

Jenna eyed him with caution. His grin was magnetic. Wonderful.

She wanted more of it.

'Say please.'

'Please,' Riley said promptly and grabbed—and the first mouthful went down before Jenna even managed to smile. He tasted and his eyes widened in astonishment.

'Wow!'

'Don't you want your beans?'

'No way.' He devoured another forkful and then another. 'I'm thinking I might put a lock on the door and keep you here for ever. Silly girl to get off the train. Now you have a job for life.'

A job for life.

She didn't answer. Suddenly her laughter died. She forced herself to keep on eating, but his words had hit an exposed nerve. The light-hearted banter she'd been indulging in was a camouflage.

She ate on, but she couldn't stop thinking. A job for life.

What was she going to do now? How could she cope?

Riley had suggested keeping her here—locking the door—and there was nothing stopping him doing just that. Would Brian look for his daughter? Would her own father care?

No one would.

And Nicole was dead.

She looked up and found Riley's eyes were on her, gently questioning. His grin had disappeared. 'I won't, you know,' he told her.

'You won't?'

'Keep you here.' He smiled again, but now his smile was one of disarming gentleness. 'You know, if I could take you to Adelaide I would. But in four days I'll put you on the train and you'll be safe. You'll be safe while you're here as well. You can trust me, Jenna.'

It was a totally uncalled-for gesture of reassurance and it floored her. She'd landed herself on this man with her own stupidity, and he was being so...so nice.

There was a lump forming in the back of her throat and she fought it back. She'd last cried...when? She couldn't remember. She never cried and she wasn't about to now.

'This Brian,' he said, seeing her distress, and leading her away from it. 'Karli's father. He was on the train?'

'Yes.'

'If he looks at a map he'll see how much danger you're in.'

'He won't look at a map,' she said dully. 'He's achieved his ends. He won't be thinking of us at all.'

Riley finished his dinner, looked at his empty plate with regret, and pushed back his chair with an air of a man who had all night to listen. 'Do you want to tell me about it?'

'Not much.'

'If I'm to help…'

'There's nothing more you can do to help,' she told him. 'You're doing enough.'

He hesitated. 'Then tell me because I want to know,' he said softly. 'You had a reason for getting off that train and I want to know what it was.'

'We should never have been on it.'

'So why were you?'

'Nicole sent us tickets.' She bit her lip. 'Or I thought Nicole sent us tickets.'

'Nicole?'

'My mother. Karli's mother.'

His eyes didn't leave her face. 'The lady who died yesterday. Are you going to explain?'

She sighed. She hauled his plate towards her and made to get up, but his hand shot across the table and caught her wrist. His hold was strong, yet gentle. Urgent yet patient.

'Tell me, Jenna.'

There was nothing else to do. She needed this man's help. She had to tell him.

'Nicole Razor is…was my mother,' she said and watched his eyes widen.

'Nicole Razor. The lead singer for Skyrazor?'

'That's the one,' she said grimly. 'Ex-singer, ex-model, ex-drug addict, ex-anything else you want to name.'

'I remember. She used to be married to…' He hesitated and she saw his eyes widen as he hit memory recall and got the connection. '…Charles Svenson.'

'Racing driver. Yep. That's my dad.'

'But he's not Karli's dad?'

'Karli's father was Nicole's fourth marriage—Charles was the first. Brian was probably her biggest mistake. She married him while she was high on drugs and he hooked into her for what he could get.' She hesitated. 'Though it's not fair to say he was her only mistake. All her husbands were after Nicole because of the fame thing.'

'So you're wealthy,' he said slowly and she watched as his face changed. 'You're the daughter of Charles Svenson and Nicole Razor.'

What was she supposed to say to that? She'd learned early never to say anything. But he was waiting for her to respond.

With what? With sick humour—her only defence.

'Poor little rich girl,' she said mockingly, but his face stayed still and watchful.

'So what happened?' he asked.

'Like Karli said—Nicole died yesterday.'

'I don't understand any of this.'

'It's easy.' She hesitated. 'No. It's hard, but I'll make it brief. Nicole didn't want me and she didn't want Karli. We were mistakes. Brian didn't want Karli either, but, by the time they split, he and Nicole hated each other. The court gave Nicole custody and Nicole responded by putting Karli straight into an English boarding-school.'

'Boarding-school.' Riley's brows snapped down. 'What—at five?'

'There are very few places now that take them that young,' Jenna said bitterly. 'You have to pay through the nose. And Nicole did. She was always touring, and the attraction of an English boarding-school was that it was in England. Brian is Australian. He couldn't get near Karli. Nicole was playing at custody battles to try and hurt him further.'

It was history playing over, she thought bitterly. Her own father was American and Nicole had done exactly the same thing to her.

'Hell.'

'It was hell,' Jenna whispered, but she couldn't tell him why she knew exactly what a hell it really was. 'I haven't been in contact with my mother for years, but when I found out about Karli I realised her school was only an hour's drive from where I work. I've been taking her home with me as much as I could. I just hated leaving her there.'

'Why didn't you take her permanently?'

Her eyes flashed up to his then. There was condemnation in his tone. Condemnation!

She wasn't going to explain why. How dared he even begin to think of judging her?

Their eyes locked for a moment, anger meeting anger, but his eyes softened first. A duel over the dinner plates obviously wasn't on the agenda. 'So how did you get here?' he asked, obviously deciding to let his last question go unanswered.

'Brian rang me,' she said, trying to swallow her anger and move on. 'I'd never met Brian. A lot of the stuff I've been telling you about him I've only realised in the last few days. I hadn't seen my mother for years and all I knew of her I read in the tabloids. I knew there'd been a custody battle for Karli and he'd lost, but that was all I knew. Anyway, I'd taken Karli out of school for the half-term holiday. Brian rang the school and they said she was with me. So he rang me. He said Nicole was in Australia. In Perth. I'd read in the paper that she was on tour so it made sense.'

His eyes were non-judgemental again. Watchful. 'So you decided to come and see her?'

'No one just pops in to visit Nicole.' She hesitated, trying to remember the jumble of emotions she'd felt as Brian had rung. 'But it was strange. Brian sounded really upset. He said Nicole was suffering from depression—which didn't surprise me. She was always suffering from something, and after the life she'd led and the pills she'd popped a bit of depression would be the least of it. Anyway he said she wanted to see both of us and she was prepared to pay all expenses if we came immediately.'

'So you came.'

'I didn't want to,' she told him. 'I mean…why would I want to see Nicole? I haven't had anything to do with her for years. But Brian wanted Karli over here, and seeing Nicole was ill it was Brian who was making decisions on Karli's behalf. If I didn't come then she'd have to fly out on her own. And then Brian added further incentive. The train ride.'

'Why the train?'

'The story he gave was that this was too good a chance to miss,' she told him. 'Brian's very plausible. He said he was desperately missing Karli and if we came by plane to Sydney and then had over three days travelling by train to Perth, not only would it be an exciting holiday for both of us, but it'd give him a chance to be with his daughter for a while.' She hesitated, trying to remember why she'd agreed.

'It sounded reasonable,' she told him, thinking it through. 'I knew Nicole would move heaven and earth to keep Karli and Brian apart. If someone didn't do what Nicole wanted she could be…spiteful. So if this was a chance for Karli to be in Australia, then it made sense that Brian would be grateful for the opportunity to spend some time with her. Anyway, as I said, I didn't want to come—but when I told Karli what was about to happen she disintegrated. In the end I couldn't let her travel by herself. So I agreed. That was the start of my dopiness. It was all a huge, huge mistake, and it was based on an outright lie.'

There was a moment's pause. Riley's eyes rested on her face and she sensed that he could almost see the pain. 'Tell me,' he said gently. 'Why was it a mistake?'

She felt sick. Telling him like this…it brought it all back and she felt the emotions of the last couple of days rise to the point where they almost overwhelmed her. But she forced herself to continue.

'Brian was insistent that we come straight away,' she told him. 'He said he only had a few days off work, and Nicole would maybe leave Perth or change her mind and we'd miss the opportunity. So we came. He met us at Sydney airport and whisked us straight to the train. And he was nice. He was really nice. Right up until the moment we got on the train he was nice—and then he let it all drop.'

'So what happened?'

'He started drinking,' she said. 'And when he'd had a few drinks he was cruel. Not cruel to me. To me he was just plain slimy. He couldn't keep his hands off me. But he spent the entire train journey putting Karli down. I couldn't believe it. A grown man belittling a five-year-old, over and over again.' She looked up at him, willing him to understand. 'You've met Karli. Anyone can see that she's fragile. She's the loveliest little girl, but she couldn't do anything right. It was almost as if Brian wanted to seduce me—as if he could, the slime ball—and he thought Karli was in the way.'

'But you were stuck with him,' Riley said, and she nodded.

'Yep. We were stuck on the train and couldn't get away. I thought of getting off the train when we went through Adelaide but...' She hesitated. How to say she had no money to fly them to Perth? Their flight home was paid from Perth. Their train fare was paid for. She'd decided they'd just have to stick with it.

But she wasn't going to tell Riley that.

'But I didn't,' she told him, flatly, no longer caring what he thought. 'So we travelled for another half a day and then the conductor handed Brian a message that had just been radioed through as urgent.'

He knew what she was going to say before she said it. 'Saying Nicole was dead?'

'Saying Nicole was dead,' she said flatly. 'The depression thing was a lie. And I hadn't checked.'

'So, what was it?'

'She'd taken a drug overdose,' she said, her voice flat and lifeless. 'We didn't know. But Brian knew. She went into a coma five days ago and she'd been on life support ever since.'

He frowned. 'But—'

'Nicole has no family,' Jenna told him. 'Apart from me and Karli and we…we've never counted. But apparently there was some glitch in the divorce proceedings with Brian, which Brian's kept quiet about and hoped like crazy that Nicole didn't realize. So he's still officially her husband. Maybe he guessed with her lifestyle there was a good chance she'd soon end up dead. Anyway, he's planned this from the time he knew her condition was hopeless. He stopped the hospital leaking her condition to the press. He got us both out here and as soon as he had us safely on the train he gave permission for her life support to be turned off.'

There was a long silence. Then… 'I still don't understand.'

He didn't understand? She barely did herself. She lifted her water glass, twisted it round and round as if by doing so maybe she could see things from a different angle. Suddenly Riley's hand came across the table to rest on hers, forcing the glass down. She released the glass, but his hand stayed where it was. Warm and strong and compelling.

'Tell me.'

She had to tell him. She had to say it out loud.

'It was because of Nicole's will,' she whispered.

'What about Nicole's will?'

'I'm only going on what Brian yelled at me,' she told him. 'But as far as I understand... When Nicole married Brian she made a will leaving him everything, but then she started hating Brian as much as she hated my father.' She hesitated, trying to make clear something that had no logic—that only unreasoned malice could explain. 'All through my childhood—and Karli's—Nicole worked very hard to get us both away from our respective fathers, so much so that we've been permanently based in England. I know she's thought of that as a success. Charles is in America. Brian's in Australia. Karli and I are in England and if there's ever been a suggestion that we go anywhere else then Nicole's almost been apoplectic with rage.'

He nodded, trying to take it in. 'And so?'

'So the codicil said that as long as Karli and I were still in England when she died and we had no contact with our fathers, then we'd inherit everything she owns. Which, I gather, is a fortune. But it seems that the rough way the change was drafted means that as Karli and I weren't in England at the exact time of her death, then the original will stays valid, and Brian gets everything.'

His eyes darkened. She could see anger flaring.

'So he conned you into leaving England.'

'For myself I don't care,' she whispered. 'But the way it happened was awful. Brian came into the lounge car on the train and everyone was there. An old lady was telling Karli a story about the Koori people who lived out here. Karli was happy. Just for a minute she was happy. Then Brian appeared. He walked straight up to Karli and he put his face into hers and he shouted ''Your mother's dead and you'll get nothing. I've won. You stupid little brat, you won't get a thing''.'

'No.' It was a whispered exclamation of horror that she could only agree with.

'So I got off the train,' she said dully. 'There was nothing else I could do. Karli went limp with shock and I picked her up and took her back to our compartment and started throwing our stuff into our suitcases—fast, because the train was already stopped. Just as it started moving we got off. End of story. Brian's gone on to Perth to claim Nicole's fortune, and Karli and I... Karli and I are going home.'

Home.

Home to what? Home to her bleak little bedsitter. Home with Karli. There'd be no money for school fees now. Karli would have to live with her.

Maybe that was for the best anyway.

Maybe she could sue Nicole's estate for Karli's maintenance, she thought drearily, and then reality slammed back again. Yeah, right. As if she could afford a lawyer.

And she still had to get them home. She had to get to Perth so she could use their return plane tickets. How much would it cost to get them from here to Perth? Were their train tickets still valid?

It was all just too hard. Despite the heat, Jenna suddenly felt cold. She gave a long, convulsive shudder, then pulled her hand away from Riley's and started to rise. She lifted a plate, but Riley was before her, rising and taking the plate from her.

'Leave it,' he told her. 'I'll handle the washing-up. Seeing you cooked, it's only fair. You go and take a shower. I'll clean up and make coffee.'

'Coffee?'

'It's my one skill,' he said with pride. 'My coffee's the best for miles.'

'That's not saying much,' Jenna retorted, responding to the gentle smile in his eyes. He was encouraging her to lighten—and there was something about this man that did just that. He made her smile when smiling seemed impossible. 'There's nothing but saltbush for miles. Unless your cows make coffee.'

'Don't disparage my skills. You wait. And mean-while...' He turned and delved into a crate by the door, rising with an armful of linen. 'Here you go, Miss Svenson. Don't let it be said that Barinya Downs doesn't provide its guests with luxury.' At her look of amazement he grinned. 'Maggie packs this for me, in case I ever want to change my sheets—which, I'll admit, doesn't happen so much as she hopes.' His smile deepened. 'You know where the shower is—you saw me come out of it. It works on bore water. You need to pump while you shower. Cold water only. And you found the toilet? I should have warned you that you need to watch out for spiders. Take the torch, and if you get bitten make sure it's somewhere I can put a tourniquet.'

'You're kidding.'

He relented. 'I'm kidding. There was a redback spider nest when I arrived, so I did the hero thing with a can of insecticide.' He eyed her clothes. 'You want something to sleep in?'

'I guess.' She'd put Karli to bed in her knickers, but knickers were hardly appropriate nightwear for her. She was practically sharing a bedroom here. 'I left our gear on the siding.'

'Very wise.' He smiled again. 'The good thing about being the only humans for a hundred miles is that no one's going to pinch your designer luggage.'

Designer luggage? What did he think she was? She tried a glower but she was too tired and too confused and too…just too everything. The day was suddenly on top of her and he could see it.

'I'll put one of my shirts around the wash-house door,' he told her, taking pity on her sudden confusion. He placed a hand on her shoulder—gently, reassuringly. It was the sort of gesture he might have used on Karli, and why it suddenly made her want to weep she had no idea.

'Go take your shower, Jenna,' he told her. 'Worry about tomorrow tomorrow. For tonight, I think we all need to sleep.'

She definitely wanted to sleep, but she also definitely wanted to shower.

She made up the bed at the far end of the veranda and lifted Karli over. The little girl didn't wake as she was shifted. Her tummy was full, she felt safe and cared for, and her body was taking all the sleep it needed.

Karli still had a child's ability to sleep whenever she needed. Jenna wasn't quite so lucky. Dust was ingrained in every pore, and the thought of cold running water was even more appealing than sleep.

Maybe she shouldn't shower when the little girl was alone, she thought briefly, but Karli was deeply asleep. Even if she stirred... Jenna thought of Riley's tone as he'd talked to Karli. The way he'd smiled and the way Karli had responded.

'You're nice,' Karli had whispered. 'Nicer than my daddy.'

Karli was right. Jenna acknowledged it as truth, using a sixth sense that years of coping with an unkind world had taught her to trust. Riley Jackson was kind, with an ingrained sense of decency she knew she could depend on.

She could depend on him?

'I can,' she whispered. The man might make her senses come alive as they'd never come alive before; he might make her feel as aware as she'd ever been aware of a man—but she knew that here in his house she'd found a haven for her little sister that she could trust absolutely.

So, yes, she could take a shower. The concept was even appealing when she examined the wash house.

It was definitely a wash house, she decided. Calling this place a bathroom would be a joke. The ramshackle lean-to at the side of the house consisted of four walls, a concrete floor and a pipe with a shower-rose at head height. Beside the pipe was a pump. If one pumped, Jenna guessed, the water would spray out over her head.

The only problem was that the pump was designed for someone with muscles like Riley Jackson.

Jenna stripped and pumped. And pumped. And pumped. The water trickled out, grudgingly.

'There's nothing like building up a sweat as you shower,' she told herself as she tried to pump and lather at the same time. 'No wonder the man has muscles.'

'Are you talking to yourself or do you have company?'

She froze. Naked and soapy, she crossed her arms uselessly across her breasts. The door had no lock—of course—and part of Jenna expected Riley to walk straight in.

'I'm okay,' she quavered.

'Hey, it's all right.' He'd heard her fear, she thought, and, damn, there was suddenly laughter behind his concern. 'We colonists know not to intrude on a lady's ablutions. Even though you imperialists do wander round strange men's bedrooms at will.'

Damn the man, he was laughing at her! 'Oh, go away,' she snapped. She shoved the pump handle down so hard that a thoroughly satisfactory stream of water gushed down over her hot-and-bothered body. That was all it needed. Anger. Well, if that was all it needed, she had anger by the bucketload. 'I can't concentrate with you out there,' she told him, pumping with a vengeance, and she could hear his grin broaden.

'Do you need to concentrate?'

'Yes,' she snapped. 'I can't handle the soap and the pump at the same time. This pump was built for Superman.'

'You want me to come in and help?'

'No!' It was a yelp and there was a broad chuckle from outside the door. Which, strangely enough, seemed reassuring. Then the door opened a crack and Jenna went back to clutching her breasts. But all that appeared was a tanned, sinewy arm, holding a shirt. The arm reached up and hooked the shirt behind the door—and then the arm retreated.

'Never let it be said that I didn't offer,' Riley told her, sounding wounded. 'But if you don't want help, then far be it from me to push. I'm off to bed. There's coffee on your bedside table. Is there anything else you need?'

'Privacy,' she snapped, and again there was a chuckle.

'What, no thank you?'

She thought about that. Thank you. Okay, maybe he deserved one of those.

'Thank you,' she whispered and heard a sudden arrested silence on the other side of the door.

'Think nothing of it,' he said at last.

'I mean it,' she managed. It was surreal, standing naked and dripping and talking to a complete stranger on the other side of the door. But she had to say it. 'Without you we'd be in desperate trouble,' she told him. 'We're incredibly grateful. Both of us.'

'Yeah,' he said, and the laughter was suddenly gone from his voice. 'Yeah, well, that's just fine. Goodnight.'

And he left her to it.

He left her disconcerted to say the least. She pumped on, but she was thoroughly confused.

Why did he have this effect on her? Despite the cold water, her body seemed to be burning. The man had her unnerved, and it wasn't just the strangeness and isolation that were making her jumpy.

It was the way her body reacted to him, she decided. It was as if he had the power to flick a switch inside her, making her achingly aware of herself—of nerve endings she'd never imagined she had.

Which was really, really dumb. She was here with Karli. As well as looking out for herself, she now had to look after a child. The responsibility was almost overpowering.

The last thing she needed to do was to complicate her life by pretending she was attracted to some yahoo cowboy in the Australian Outback.

Pretending?

'Okay, so you're attracted,' she conceded. 'But you're not stupid. Now stop fantasising and get your hair washed and get out of here.'

Even that was easier said than done. Jenna's hair was full of dust, but there was no shampoo and the soap refused to lather. No matter how she scrubbed, there were no suds. Finally she pumped the soap out, but her hair still felt stiff and matted.

At least the worst of the dust had gone, and without Riley's disturbing presence her body was finally cool. She towelled herself dry, put on Riley's shirt—it hung almost to her knees—and tried to run a comb through her hair.

She winced at the feel. Why wasn't it clean? Puzzled, she pumped a little water into her hand and tasted. It was thick with salts—coarse, untreated bore water.

At least the tap in the kitchen was connected to rainwater, she decided. She could rinse her hair there.

She retrieved her kerosene lamp from the corner of the wash house, gathered her belongings and took a cautious step back onto the veranda.

Riley was already in bed.

There was a hump under the bedclothes on his end of the veranda and he didn't stir as she came out. She thought back to the man's face as she'd first seen him. One of her first impressions had been exhaustion. 'I've been working in the sun for the past twelve hours,' he'd told her.

He deserved his sleep.

Well, she wouldn't disturb him. She checked on Karli, who was also sleeping soundly, dumped her filthy clothes at the foot of the bed she'd be sharing with her sister, drank her coffee—which tasted surprisingly good—then tiptoed past Riley and back out to the kitchen.

Here was the rainwater. She gave a sigh of relief, turned on the tap and lowered her head under its flow. And let it run...

'What the hell do you think you're doing?'

She bumped her head on the tap. She gasped, got a mouthful of water and choked. When she finally managed to raise her head, Riley was towering above her. The tap was firmly turned off and it didn't take a genius to see that he was angry. More than angry. He was full-blown furious.

'What…?' Jenna tried to talk, coughed and tried again. 'What do you mean?' The man was dressed only in a pair of boxer shorts. He was almost as naked as Jenna felt. In Riley's shirt, bra-less and with no knickers, she felt exposed and…and…

Well, just plain exposed.

'Bloody English twit.' Riley placed his hands on Jenna's arms and physically lifted her away from the tap. Then he tilted her chin, forcing her to face him. 'Lady, there is one fact of life you learn here and you learn it fast. There is nothing—nothing!—more precious than rainwater. Rain water is the only thing we can drink and it hasn't rained for six months. And here you are, letting it run all over your hair and down the drain. I reckon you've just used two weeks' drinking water.'

'But…' Jenna's voice faltered into appalled horror '…are you so short?'

'Short enough that a couple more hair washes will make the place uninhabitable.'

Jenna stared up at him in the flickering light cast by her lantern. She was appalled. 'I'm so sorry.'

'You'll be a lot sorrier if you die of thirst,' he said grimly. 'All for the sake of clean hair.'

Silence.

'The cattle…' she managed. 'How do they survive?'

'They have a stronger tolerance for salts than we do. They'll drink bore water.'

'Oh, help.'

'Help's right.' He stared down at her for a moment longer. And then, before she realised what he intended, before she could possibly react, he bent and lifted her into his arms, tossing her against his bare chest as if she weighed nothing.

'What...what are you doing?' Jenna squeaked. 'Put me down.'

'You, Miss Svenson, have caused enough trouble for one day,' Riley said grimly, only the sides of his mouth twitching as though he was suppressing laughter. 'You may have come from a privileged background where everything you wanted you got, but there are rules in this place and you obey them or you pay the consequences.' And holding her effortlessly against him, he stooped to turned down her lamp and then strode out to the veranda.

She held herself rigid in his grasp. There was nothing she could do except clutch her dignity to herself as best she could and submit. She couldn't fight him. If she wriggled...well, Riley's shirt was making her respectable but only just, and there wasn't a lot of wriggle room.

But, the feel of this man's arms, of this man's skin against hers... What was happening to her?

She trusted him, she told herself fiercely. She trusted him and her instincts weren't wrong. Were they?

'What are you doing?' she managed as he kicked the door open before him and made his way unerringly through the darkened house.

'I'm doing what everyone does with misbehaving juveniles,' he told her, with only a hint of wicked laughter in his voice. 'I'm sending you to bed.'

He strode on with her speechless, rigid in his grasp.

Finally he reached the bed on the veranda. Karli was sound asleep on one side, barely taking up any room at all. Riley stood, looked down at the sleeping little girl in the moonlight and his face twisted.

'You're nothing but trouble,' he told Jenna. 'The two of you.'

He held her out over her side of the bed and let her drop. She landed with an ignominious bounce.

He lifted a spare towel from the pile of linen beside the bed and he dropped it onto her head.

'If I were you, I'd towel myself dry, then get into bed and stay there,' he told her. 'And if I catch you wasting rainwater again, then I will personally place you in the Land Rover and take you to the railway siding and leave you there until the next train comes through.' He glanced across at Karli and once again his mouth twisted. His expression was one that almost might have been pain.

'I should do it now,' he muttered. 'I can't, of course, but I should.'

He stood for a moment, still staring down, only now he was staring at Jenna, as if he was expecting her to defy him.

She didn't. She couldn't. She lay staring up at him in the moonlight and she was absolutely speechless.

And Riley's mouth quirked into a rueful smile.

'Goodnight, then, Miss Svenson,' he said softly. His hand came down and he touched her face—fleetingly, in a gesture that was as unexpected as it was comforting. 'Sleep well. Don't let the traffic keep you awake.'

And he was gone, striding purposefully back to his own bed as if rid of a pest. To her fury, as she heard him lower himself onto his bed she heard a low, throaty chuckle.

Angry or not, Riley Jackson had just enjoyed himself.

Toad!

For ten minutes she lay still, her face burning with mortification. She was also trying to block out the knowledge that Riley was in bed not fifteen feet away from her.

She sat up and towelled her hair, turned her pillow to the dry side, then lay and stared in the opposite direction to Riley, out into the night sky.

Facing away from him didn't help a bit.

She was a fool. What must he think of her? From the moment she'd left the train she'd been nothing but a twit, and she should have guessed about the water.

'Let it go,' Riley growled and she almost jumped sky-high.

'I'll get over it and so will you,' he told her, his voice weirdly intimate in the night. They were lying in the same bedroom like two lovers and his words were so soft that she almost might have been dreaming.

'I…thank you,' she whispered and once again she heard the chuckle.

'You're welcome. Go to sleep.'

Sleep. How could she sleep? She wriggled down between the sheets and lay rigid. Karli slept on beside her, calmly oblivious of the turmoil her big sister was experiencing.

It'd be great to be five years old, Jenna thought bitterly, and then she thought of what she'd gone through from that age until now and thought, no. No, it wouldn't.

She put out her hand and took Karli's in hers. The little girl's fingers curled around hers, trusting even in sleep.

She'd do whatever it took, Jenna thought. Whatever…

Damn Brian.

Men!

She'd never sleep.

She wriggled down further into the bed. Amazingly, the mattress and pillows were comfortable. 'Not that it'll make a scrap of difference,' she told herself. 'There's no way I can sleep here.'

Her damp curls sank deeper into the pillow. The warm night air caressed her tired body, soothing her fears. Beyond the veranda, the stars were brilliant in the outback sky.

Karli held her hand, and Riley was asleep close by.

'There's no way I can sleep here,' she repeated, but the words grew slower as she thought them. 'There's no way.'

The world was still.

Her eyes closed.

She slept.

CHAPTER FOUR

HE LEFT at dawn.

Riley had work crowding in on him from all sides. He was desperate to be gone, but first he turned his battered truck towards the railway siding. They'd need their abandoned baggage and he didn't want them trying to get it themselves.

He slowed as he reached the siding. He pulled up on the south side, where there was a little shade from a sun that already had a sting to it. What on earth was this?

He climbed from the truck and stared.

Sandcastles? Dust-castles? What?

The edifices were amazing. They—Jenna and Karli, for who else could have done this?—had built an entire little town. There were scores of little dust houses, made of packed-together dirt, adorned with twigs from the saltbush to form windows and doors and chimneys. There were roads in their little village and a scooped-out something that might be meant to resemble a pond. There were a couple of little twiggy things in the middle of the pond and he stooped to see.

Ducks. They'd fashioned ducks in the desert. He shook his head in stunned amazement.

He'd imagined them sitting bereft on the platform until it was cool enough to try and walk to the house.

He'd imagined wrong.

Jenna wasn't a lady who'd take kindly to the label *bereft*, he thought. She was some woman!

Stop thinking of Jenna, he told himself, and suddenly the voice inside his head was harsh. Get on with what needs to be done.

But harsh command or not, he turned from the ducks with reluctance.

Who else would sit in the dust and make ducks? Ridiculous.

Their gear was right where they'd left it, a mute testament to their desperation in leaving the train. There was one designer suitcase—that was what he'd expected—a gorgeous affair in pink leather with Karli's name embossed on the side.

The other suitcase, however, had him intrigued all over again. The ancient box of a thing looked as if it was barely holding together.

So this was why Jenna had reacted with grim humour when he'd suggested she had designer baggage. He loaded the cases into the truck and drove back to the house, trying to figure things out.

Jenna was Nicole Razor's daughter. Charles Svenson was her father. He'd heard of Nicole and of Charles.

Until her death Nicole had been depicted in the media as a wasted, ageing rock star. The tabloids said she spent half of her life out of it on drugs.

Charles Svenson had the same high media profile, but as far as Riley knew the man was still healthy, wealthy and in the public eye. He'd been an incredibly successful Formula One driver.

Once, a long time ago, Riley's father had taken a small Riley to a Grand Prix race. Charles Svenson had stood on the winner's podium, and Riley's father had grimaced in disgust. 'I can't applaud him,' he'd told his son. 'Svenson's a fine driver but his morals would put a sewer rat to shame.'

The eight-year-old Riley had been shocked. Riley's father hadn't spoken ill of anyone unless really pushed, so for him that had been quite an indictment. His comment had stuck. As a small boy, Riley had plastered his room with posters of Formula One drivers, but from that moment Charles Svenson had been conspicuous by his absence.

Jenna was his daughter.

It had been a long time since Svenson had driven a racing car, Riley thought grimly, but his reputation was still of a womaniser living on the edge of a corrupt world. He couldn't imagine what it must be like to be his child. In truth, Nicole and Charles created a combination of parenthood that no one would want.

But at least Jenna should have money. It was inconceivable that she didn't.

She'd be another Lisa, he told himself as he hauled their suitcases into the house, but then he looked again at the battered suitcase, and he thought of the twiggy little ducks and felt that same tug of doubt. Then he reached the veranda and looked down at Jenna's face as she slept—and the tug grew stronger.

Jenna was cuddling her little sister. Karli was curled against her and Jenna's grip was protective even in sleep. She looked almost fierce.

Maybe if he'd met the unspeakable Brian, he'd feel like that too.

But he wouldn't meet Karli's father. Why would he? He had nothing to do with this pair. On Monday they'd be on the train and out of here.

Still unsettled, he went back to the kitchen, foraged around until he found a few cans of orange juice that he'd vaguely remembered Maggie lecturing him about, then took a can and two glasses back to the bedroom. He stared at the sleeping woman and child for a moment longer.

This was useless. He was getting involved.

He didn't get involved.

Get out of here, he told himself. Now.

And he turned and went before he could talk himself out of it.

Jenna woke to silence.

She opened her eyes and surveyed the world with caution. The searing heat of the day hadn't yet blasted in, but it was well after sunrise. Jenna could see for miles, the land to the horizon stark and arid in the morning light.

The wind had dropped. The dust clouds of yesterday were no longer sweeping the paddocks. She closed her eyes with relief, wiggling her toes against the clean linen and thinking of what could have happened if Riley hadn't been here.

He had been here. The nightmare hadn't happened.

'Are you awake yet, Jenna?'

She turned and her sister's small face was right against hers. Karli was cuddling in, enjoying the warmth and comfort of her newly acquired big sister. It had taken Jenna months to get the little girl to trust her but now, as far as Karli was concerned, Jenna could do no wrong.

'I'm awake, sweetie. Hush. You'll wake Mr Jackson.'

'He's gone.'

Gone. She stared over her little sister's head.

The bed at the far end of the veranda was empty.

'His truck drove away,' Karli said, and Jenna frowned.

'When?'

'Just then. He drove away and then he came back, but he's gone again now. I pretended to be asleep. He put something beside our bed and then he stood and looked at us, but he didn't say anything.'

For heaven's sake. How deeply had she been sleeping?

She pushed her sheet aside and rose, but with care. Whether or not Riley was gone, she wasn't taking chances. She checked the buttons on her makeshift nightshirt—and then examined the evidence.

Riley's bed was made. His work clothes, which had been strewn on the chair beside his bed the previous night, were gone as well.

On the floor beside their own bed, Jenna saw two suitcases. Sitting on top were two glasses and a can of orange juice.

'Hey, he's brought us our clothes,' she told Karli, and it was strange how different she suddenly felt. It was a small gesture, she thought, driving across to the siding to fetch their gear and then bringing them orange juice, but it felt…great. It felt as if he cared.

Having someone care was a sensation Jenna hadn't felt for a long time. If ever. She stared down at the suitcases and felt the beginnings of a lump form in her throat.

'Orange juice,' Karli said and hopped out of bed. 'Cool. I didn't know it came in cans.'

Jenna found herself smiling. 'I bet that was Maggie's idea as well,' she said as Karli lifted the can and inspected it from all angles.

'Who's Maggie?'

'I have no idea,' Jenna said. 'But I think she's a friend.'

But Karli had lost interest. 'He's really gone.' She pulled the ring top and poured two glasses of orange juice with meticulous care. 'I'll pour and you choose.'

Jenna watched, chose, and then they sat on the bed and drank their orange juice, two co-conspirators in some exciting plan. That was what it felt like, Jenna thought. For the first time since she'd left England she felt a tiny frisson of excitement. Anticipation even. This was an adventure.

And Riley had brought them orange juice.

Riley had nothing to do with it, she told herself crossly. It was just the combination of events and the lessening of anxiety. This was the Australian Outback. They were safe. In three days they'd get on the train and they'd never see anything like this ever again—so they might as well enjoy themselves.

Their mother was dead.

The thought flashed home with a sickening jolt and she felt a stab of remorse. She was feeling happy—light—and Nicole was dead.

She could hardly feel sorrow, though. Karli had reacted to the news with shock and with fear, but it was because of the way Brian had thrown it at her. And it had been only eight months since Nicole had sent Karli away. Karli still had some concept of Nicole as a mother, even though all the mothering had been done by the hired help. So Karli had been upset.

But for Jenna... Well, she'd been sent away at the same age as Karli. There'd been fleeting sightings when Nicole had been in England, but for Jenna they'd usually been unsettling, even frightening times. They'd been times when the school had been closed for holidays and she'd been thrust, unwanted, into a paparazzi-filled lifestyle where her mother had been sometimes gushing, sometimes vicious, but mostly totally unaware of her daughter at all.

So, no, she didn't feel sorrow for Nicole. She felt nothing.

Except freedom. And it was a freedom, she told herself. Nicole was no longer around to utter sweeping edicts such as, 'Karli is not to leave the school.' Brian didn't care about Karli. So maybe now Karli had a chance of being happy.

She grinned at the little girl. Karli looked over her glass of juice, and her eyes were huge.

'Is this an adventure?' she asked, echoing Jenna's thoughts, and Jenna grinned some more.

'I guess it is.' There was an ancient dresser at the end of the bed, with a cracked mirror above. She stared at their reflection, a rumpled little girl and a woman in an oversized man's shirt. Her reflection startled her. Her nose and arms were bright pink—waiting until late to make yesterday's trek hadn't been enough to protect her English complexion from the harsh Australian sun. Her burnt-red shoulder-length curls were sticking up every which way after going to sleep with them wet. And Karli matched.

She giggled.

'Look at us,' she told Karli.

'I'm Rudolph,' Karli decided, and giggled in return.

'So you are, Rudolph Red Nose. Two matching red-nosed tourists, stranded in the middle of the Australian Outback. How much of an adventure is that?'

Karli put her finger on her nose and squashed it, considering. 'Where do you think Mr Jackson's gone?'

'Maybe he's started work. He said something about unblocking water pipes for his cattle. Let's go see if he left any clues. Our red noses can lead the way.'

Karli giggled again, a wonderful sound.

They made their way through the house, holding hands like a treasure hunt. Or hide and seek. The thought that Riley might be just around the corner was…intriguing.

He wasn't just around the corner. The house was deserted and on the kitchen table was a note.

I have work to do on the outer edges of the property so I won't be back until tomorrow night. Make yourselves at home. Eat as many of Maggie's fancy vegetables as you like. If you're bored maybe you could do something about the dust. The house could use a good spring-clean.

The note was held down by a can of beans.

'What does it say?' Karli asked, and Jenna read it to her, trying to swallow a stupid and unbidden surge of disappointment. This was good, wasn't it? She didn't want the man here, unsettling her. She thought back to how she'd felt the night before when he'd lifted her into his arms and she knew she should be thankful that Riley was gone.

The man was dangerous.

'So what will we do?' Karli asked, and to Jenna's astonishment she heard her own disappointment echoed in Karli's voice. What was it with the man?

She gave herself a fast mental swipe and gathered her wits.

'First,' she told Karli, 'I'm going to introduce you to an amazing wash house. It's really fun. And then...' She squared her shoulders. She had no doubt that the note had been written in jest, but it was a challenge for all that. She stared around her.

'Then we're going to do some housekeeping,' she told Karli. 'You and I will teach Riley Jackson that women aren't as useless as he thinks we are. We can fix this place right up.'

Karli stared around her. 'You mean we're going to clean?'

'Yep.'

Karli looked exceedingly doubtful. 'This house is really, really dirty.'

'If it wasn't dirty, then it wouldn't need cleaning,' Jenna told her. 'And it wouldn't be fun. You know the maids in the hotels Nicole stays...stayed in?'

Karli didn't even hear the catch. 'Yes.' She screwed up her nose, remembering. 'Some of them were nice.'

'But they never looked like they were having fun, did they?'

'No.'

'That's because hotel rooms are cleaned every single day,' Jenna told her. 'They never get a chance to get dirty. Whereas this place has had a chance to get really, really dirty. So we can definitely have fun.'

'Can we?'

'Sure we can,' Jenna said, looking round her again and trying not to falter. If she sat here for two days and thought about her future—about all the difficulties she was facing as soon as she got back to the outside world—then she'd go nuts. The only way to cope was to stay busy.

'I'm good at dusting,' Karli said, though her tone said she wasn't quite sure.

'Me too,' Jenna said, and caught Karli up in a bear hug. 'That makes two of us who are excellent dusters, so it's just as well there's lots and lots of dust. Let's start now.'

He didn't want to be out here.

Why would he? It was searingly hot work, made only bearable by the queues of fragile cattle who were lined up at the troughs waiting patiently for water to start flowing again. A couple of the lines had been blocked for too long and the sights there were heartbreaking. But he'd come in time to save most of these half-dead cattle. He cleared the lines, greased machinery that hadn't seen oil for years, started the water flowing and then stood back. The gentle crossbred Brahman cattle, known locally as Droughtmasters, then took turn to put their noses into the precious water, as if they had all the time in the world to wait and this weren't a drink that their lives depended on.

Mostly the lines weren't completely blocked, which was why so many of the cattle had survived for so long. But many of the troughs themselves were silted up and the cattle had been licking water off a base of sand.

'I know,' he told them as they watched him work with a patience that astounded him. 'It's bloody criminal. It's not my fault, guys. Now I own the place things will be different. I promise.'

They couldn't understand—how could they? But they watched him with eyes that had him almost swearing that they did.

The urge to leave them and go back to the house with his intriguing visitors had to be put to one side.

He worked on. It was hot, lonely, back-breaking work and he worked until the light went completely. Then he slept under the stars, tossing a swag onto the sand and collapsing onto it. He woke at dawn and his first thought was how the girls had got on back at the house.

It was no business of his.

But it niggled him. He didn't like the thought that they were alone. If one of them were to get ill…

He couldn't do anything about it, he told himself savagely. There was only one radio and he needed it. To be out here without a radio was suicidal.

But if he worked through today, then the urgent outer bores would be okay. Tomorrow and the next day he could work nearer the house. In truth, if he worked as hard today as he had yesterday then the cattle's urgent needs would be assuaged and he'd have time to draw breath.

He rolled over and flicked on the radio. There wasn't anything like cheerful tunes on any channel out here. It was for emergency contact only. But he hopped around the channels and found a signal from Finya Downs. His nearest neighbour, Bill Holmes, was trying to get in touch. He tuned in, and Bill came on air straight away.

Bill was over seventy. He and his wife, Dot, had a homestead a hundred miles to the north. They kept themselves absolutely to themselves and Riley frowned as he tuned in. There'd have to be an urgent need for Bill to try and reach him.

'Hey, Jackson.' Bill was a man of few words and he didn't waste them now. 'I saw you pick up stuff from the train on Thursday and guessed you might still be there. You found any stray passengers?'

That was to the point. Riley thought about it. 'I might have,' he said cautiously, and Bill's voice cracked into laughter.

'Right. You're a man after me own heart. Don't let anything on until you know what I'm on about. But you've got the girl and the kiddy safe?'

'Um…yeah.'

'They'd be bloody lucky, eh?'

'How do you know about them?'

'Doug Stanley of the Territory police's been on the wire. Doug doesn't know there's anyone at your place, of course, so I'm the nearest he could think of to contact. Seems someone on the train saw a woman and a guy fighting, the guy yelling at a kid, and the woman getting upset. They're thinking the woman and the kid got off the train at the siding too late for the train staff to notice. But some old duck on the train noticed—Enid O'Connell. She used to be a chief magistrate. She kicked up a fuss and finally the conductor contacted the police. So Doug radioed me. I told Doug I was at the siding picking up supplies and no one got off. Or no one that I saw. But most of us left before the train pulled out. Your place is the only place within walking distance. If you hadn't seen them, then they're talking of starting a search.'

'I've got 'em.'

'Thank God for that, then,' Bill said bluntly. 'Otherwise they'd have stayed on the siding all yesterday and they'd have cooked. If you weren't there, the missus said I had to drive back over to the siding and check.'

'They're safe. They'll get back on the train on Monday.'

'You'll let the coppers know?'

'I'll do that straight away.'

Bill hesitated.

'Seems they're some bloody rock star's kids,' he said, reluctantly as if he was being prompted from behind. 'Nicole someone's the mother, and my missus says she's loopy. Drugs and some such. Anyway she's dead of an overdose and Doug says it's all over the papers.'

Riley winced at that. 'I'd imagine it might be.'

'Doug's saying it's gonna be a big beat up. Dead rock star's daughters missing in the desert.'

'Mmm.'

'There'll be a fuss when they get on the train.'

'Yeah.'

'Anyway…' Bill cleared his throat. 'No business of mine. You tell the cops they're okay and I'll reassure the missus. It'll keep everyone off our backs.'

'Fine.'

'Jackson?'

'Yeah?'

'Glad you bought the place,' Bill said, a trifle roughly. And then, unexpectedly: 'There's about two hundred head of your cattle I sort of steered to my side of the boundary rather than let them die of thirst. I might steer them back now.'

Riley grinned. Well, well. 'That's good of you.'

'What are neighbours for?' Once more Bill hesitated. 'Just…when this business is all over can you radio the missus and tell her what the hell this is all about? Otherwise I'll never hear the end of it.'

Riley's grin deepened. He knew Dot. The thought of a girl and a child stranded on the siding would be almost too much for her. She'd be wanting to get in the truck and drive back herself, and Bill would have his work cut out to keep her at home.

Bill's dislike for socialising had just cost him two hundred head of cattle.

'I'll contact Dot personally,' Riley promised, and then couldn't help himself. 'And I won't even ask how long you've been "saving" my cattle for me, you thieving old poddy dodger.'

Then, as he heard Bill's squawk of indignation he replaced the handset with a smile.

His grin faded. He lay back on his swag again for a few short minutes. Taking in what had been said.

He'd admitted Jenna and Karli were with him. He'd assumed responsibility for them. He was in no doubt now that if he hadn't implied he was taking care of them, Dot would be here within hours, or, if not Dot, then the Territory police.

But he'd implied that things were under control.

And when it was over... He'd have to report to Dot.

Tell her what the hell this is all about.

'How can I tell her what the hell it's all about when I'll never know myself?' Riley asked himself, and then he sighed and reached for the radio again to contact the police.

To tell them things were under control.

Sort of.

Jenna and Karli worked for two days straight. They had a perfectly wonderful time.

And Karli bloomed.

Their times together in England had had their problems. Every chance she'd been able to, Jenna had fetched Karli home to her bedsitter near the hospital, but normally she'd only been able to manage twenty-four hours off duty. By the time they'd finished the long trip home, Karli had already been remembering she'd have to go back. She'd never completely relaxed.

She'd never treated Jenna as someone who might be permanent.

But now, in this incongruous setting, there was suddenly no end in sight. Sure, they were due to catch a train on Monday but that was with Jenna. Tomorrow Karli didn't have to go back to school. Jenna didn't have to go back to work. And now there was no Brian threatening, and no Nicole at the end of the journey, ready to gush or rant or ignore.

With such freedom, house-cleaning seemed an adventure to be savoured. Every time Jenna demanded rest, Karli put her hands on her hips, fixed her with a slave-driver's look and said: 'But there's still more dust.'

There certainly was, but it didn't deter them. They mapped out a plan and worked methodically through.

They blocked the two bedrooms off, judging the whole house was beyond their capabilities. The rest of the house they sealed. Apart from the doors and windows in the lee of the wind, they covered every broken window, they stuffed every crack and they sealed it so not one speck of dust could enter.

Then they cleaned.

They removed dust by the bucketload, Jenna sweeping it from higher surfaces to lower ones, Karli coming behind her and sweeping it to the floor. Then they mounded it in huge piles and whooshed it out into the yard.

All the furniture was dragged outside, Karli heaving as gamely as Jenna. With it gone, they filled bucket after bucket with the horrid bore water and they scrubbed.

Jenna would have stopped if Karli hated it, but Karli loved it. It was like a huge game, making an appalling house liveable.

They wore the clothes they'd worn from the train, judging them unspeakable already, and by the end of two more days they were truly disgusting. Jenna tied their hair up in rags so they looked like two aging charladies, and they giggled every time they caught sight of each other.

They certainly didn't look like Nicole Razor's daughters. If Nicole could see them she'd have kittens, Jenna thought, and the idea was enough to make her feel a real pang of sorrow. Nicole had missed out on so much, she thought as she watched Karli chewing her bottom lip in concentration as she tried to scrub her bit of kitchen floor really clean.

Living in five-star hotels might be fabulous for a while, but it wasn't really living. It didn't want to make you hug someone because you felt so good at what you were achieving—together.

And they were achieving. They worked all through Friday and slept the sleep of the truly exhausted on Friday night. They worked all day Saturday, and, to their shared amazement, as Saturday drew to a close they were starting to see the house as it might once have looked.

Someone had loved it. A long time ago someone had taken pride in this house.

The kitchen, under its grime, was painted a pretty pastel green. Hanging over the windows was a nondescript cloth, but when they washed it the cloth turned into attractive floral curtains that exactly matched the walls. The benches were washed clean and they'd scrubbed out the stove. Karli's floor gleamed.

It was as if the house were a treasure, hidden for years under ugly camouflage. The heat was almost forgotten as they grew more and more excited with their project. By the end of Saturday they were pounding the furniture and starting to drag it inside again, and the house was starting to look... welcoming?

'Enough,' Jenna decreed at six on Saturday night. She'd climbed up onto the roof and banged nails into loose tin to stop it clanging in the wind, and that had been her personal limit. Her hands were scratched, she was exhausted and even the slave-driving Karli was looking a bit wobbly. 'Enough, Karli, love. It's time to hit the pump. We've done more work than two people should have to do in one lifetime.'

'It's really pretty,' Karli said as Jenna sat down on the back step beside her. Karli had been supervising her roof-mending, and now she tucked her hand into Jenna's in a gesture that was entirely proprietary. 'I'm glad you're finished on the roof.'

'I stopped it banging.'

'Yeah,' Karli said with satisfaction. 'And I polished the doorknob.'

'We've done great.'

'Do you think Mr Jackson will come home tonight?'

'He might,' Jenna said, trying to sound as if she didn't care.

She did care. Which was...a problem?

Riley arrived just after sunset. He walked into the kitchen—and stopped dead.

Things had changed so much he had to blink to convince himself he wasn't seeing things.

For the last two days he'd been driving along the vast boundaries of his property, across mile after mile of drought-stricken country. He'd checked and repaired bores, he'd checked dams, he'd cleared troughs and he'd taken endless inventory. The dust, the silence and the monotony had seeped almost into his soul, leaving him blank and empty. And all the time, in the back of his mind had been the thought of this derelict house in such desperate need of repair, and his uninvited guests who were somehow his responsibility having to make do with living conditions that were dreadful. There'd been nothing he could do about it, but he'd felt appalling about them being here.

He'd returned home tonight with little anticipation other than a growing guilt that he was here just to refuel, shower and sleep before the endless work started again. That he'd find them despairing in the dust.

But what he'd walked into…

The place was transformed beyond belief. The lamp was lit on the kitchen table, sending out a soft, golden glow. A smell of baking—baking!—was wafting through the kitchen. The kitchen itself was gleaming. It looked clean and loved and even… pretty!

How had they done this?

Where were they?

There was a muted giggle from the back of the house. He heard a child's voice, happy and chirpy, and then Jenna's voice raised in response.

They were singing a sea shanty he vaguely recognised.

'Pull, ye land lubbers, pull.'

Fascinated, he made his way through to the wash-house door. They were both in there. He could hear their splashing and their laughter and their crazy song.

It was like coming home.

The thought was such a jolt that he felt almost as if he'd been hit in the gut. The sensation of homeliness. A child's laughter. Jenna…

She was in the shower. They were pumping together and using sea shanties to get the rhythm of the pump. They were singing and giggling and pumping and splashing—and Riley had to stand against the wall as a wave of aching need jolted through his gut so hard he thought he'd fall.

Hell!

'Enough.' It was Jenna's voice, still laughing, with a hint of spluttering. 'Out of here, you little water baby. I don't know how much bore water there is—'

'There's plenty,' he called. 'Bore water's not a problem. Splash all you want.'

There was a shocked silence from inside the wash house as they obviously heard and figured they had company. And then came Karli's voice. Joyous.

'Mr Jackson's home. Jenna, Mr Jackson's home. Mr Jackson, we're having a pump shower. Do you want a pump shower? We're really good at pumping.'

'Um... Mr Jackson needs to wait for us to finish,' Jenna said in a voice that was none too steady.

'You still don't need help with the pump?' He smiled, but his smile was crooked. Something inside him was being touched that hadn't been touched for a very long time and he wasn't sure that he appreciated the sensation.

'Karli has pumping down to a fine art,' Jenna told him.

'There's rules about child labour.'

'Don't you dare tell Karli.' She was laughing again, he decided, and he liked it. He liked it a lot. The guilt that had been with him for the last two days slipped away and he found himself grinning like a fool. 'We'll be out in a minute,' she called. 'Don't dirty our tidy house.'

'As if I would.' He was gazing the length of the veranda and they'd been busy here, too. 'What on earth have you two been doing?'

'We've been dusting,' Karli called out, proudly. The water had stopped and her voice was slightly muffled as if she was being towelled. 'Me and Jenna don't like dust.'

'You come to Barinya Downs when you don't like dust? A bit of dust does no one any harm.'

'You bring one speck into this house, Riley Jackson, and we'll hang you out like we hung out the rugs,' Jenna said darkly. 'How are your cows?'

'Better for having some water,' he told her and the feeling of domesticity deepened. What was the line wives used to their husbands? *How was your day, dear?*

Something was missing. The wind was rising, whistling round the house with the same eerie moan as it had since he'd arrived. But...

'The roof's not banging,' he said on a note of discovery.

'Jenna fixed the flapping tin,' Karli told him. It was a strange conversation, on either side of the wash-house door, crazily intimate. 'I held the ladder while she banged the nails.'

Jenna fixed the roof? 'What with?' he demanded, stunned.

'With nails,' Jenna said as if he were stupid—which was exactly how he was feeling. 'We found them in one of the sheds with a bunch of old tools. I banged forty-seven nails and one thumb. One thumb twice.'

'Ouch.'

'Ouch is right.'

'Jenna said a bad word,' Karli told him—and she giggled.

He still wasn't sure he was hearing right. He wasn't sure that he was dreaming. 'I don't believe you,' he said and the door to the wash house swung open, to reveal two girls dressed in towels. They looked amazing. Karli was hugely respectable, wrapped in a towel that reached to the floor, but Jenna's towel covered her from her breasts to her hips and only just at that. They'd plaited their hair and pinned it up so it was a coif on each of their heads. They looked a real pair, flushed and clean and mischievous, he thought. They looked really, really pleased with themselves.

So they ought if they'd achieved this.

'What don't you believe?' Jenna demanded and Riley took an instinctive step backwards.

'Um…the roof?'

'Believe it, mister,' she said darkly.

'But you're Charles Svenson's daughter.'

'Yeah, he should have been here to help, but he doesn't make a habit of doing that,' she told him. 'And I would have called a roofer, but I couldn't find a phone book. So I just had to do it myself. By the way, I wouldn't trust your ladder too much. A rung broke as I came down.' She held up a leg and motioned to a long, jagged scratch. 'It messed up my designer clothes no end. That'll cost you an extra can of beans.'

'I don't believe it,' he said again, stupidly, and Jenna sighed.

'Okay. I lied. Climb up on your rickety ladder and see for yourself that the roof is mended, but, I admit, I called in a team of roof repairers from Adelaide.'

'No, you didn't,' Karli said, puzzled, and Jenna grinned.

'No, we didn't, but we're giving Mr Jackson some pride back. He doesn't like the thought of mere women fixing his roof. You'll understand male pride—and male ego—when you're a bit older. In the meantime…' She faced Riley square on, a diminutive redhead with a towel. 'I know this sounds unreasonable, Mr Jackson, but we need to kick you out of your bedroom so we can get dressed.'

'Um…right,' he said and retreated.

What else was a man to do?

CHAPTER FIVE

RILEY needed a beer, but he didn't fetch one. Instead he prowled the house.

Every chink had been closed to the all-pervading dust. The broken windows had been boarded up, but the remaining windows had been cleaned so the light from the rising moon was filtering through.

The lanterns had been cleaned. He lit one in the sitting room and gazed around at the transformed space. The big club sofa and matching chairs were clean and big and inviting.

He didn't sit. He wasn't stupid. He was covered in dust and when a cry came from the veranda— 'Shower's free'—he made it into the wash house fast.

He was starting to feel as if he didn't belong. The feeling that this was home was weird and domestic and…threatening?

He washed and hauled on a pair of jeans, then started to go out to the kitchen—and then he hesitated.

He stopped and put on a shirt. The least he could do was to pretend he knew what civilisation was.

And when he walked into the kitchen he was pleased he had. The girls looked lovely. They were in dresses. Karli's was a cute, jonquil-yellow dress with a white sash and Jenna was wearing...

A cute sundress?

Nope, he thought, and suddenly his throat felt dry. It wasn't cute. It was a simple frock, pale green, with a scooped neck and short sleeves slit to the shoulders so her arms were almost bare. The dress clung to her waist and flared out around her hips, ending up just above her knees. It was the sort of dress you might find anywhere—you might see anywhere. But she was sort of...

Sort of what?

Her hair was still coiled in a plait on her head—she must have figured this was the only way to wear it when she couldn't wash it. She wore no make-up. Her legs were bare and she wore simple sandals.

She was as far a cry from the women he'd grown up with as he could imagine—and she took his breath away.

'Do you think we look pretty?' Karli demanded. Her voice was anxious, and Jenna looked up from the pot she was stirring, saw him in the doorway and she smiled.

His breath got taken away all over again.

'Of course he thinks we look pretty,' she said. 'We're in our party clothes, Mr Jackson.'

Thank God he'd worn a shirt.

'Um…a party?'

'It's Karli's five and three-quarter'th birthday.'

'Yeah?'

'Yeah. We found some candles, which made us think about birthdays. So we figured it out while we were dusting. Karli was in school on her fifth birthday and we couldn't be together and Karli was feeling sad about that so we thought—well, her birthday is the tenth of June and now it's the tenth of March, so today is her five and three-quarter'th birthday.'

Her eyes were sending a silent message. He didn't need it. He read the message in Karli's entire stance.

This was important.

'Well, well,' he said and smiled. 'I've come home just in time for a birthday. How about that?'

'Jenna gave me a present,' Karli told him. She opened her hand and there was a tiny soap in her palm, the sort you might find in a cheap hotel. She beamed. 'It's a baby soap. It smells like flowers. I wanted to use it in the shower but Jenna said not to waste it on your yucky water.' She wrinkled her nose. 'But that's rude.' She looked at him again, suddenly anxious. 'I'm sorry. I didn't mean to be rude. And Jenna says only special people give presents on five and three-quarter'th birthdays so you don't have to give me anything. And Jenna's made a cake.'

'A cake. Amazing.' He sat down with caution as Jenna dolloped out casserole. It smelt fantastic. 'What's this?'

'It's called Jenna's Surprise,' she told him. 'While we were cleaning your cupboards we found more cans. Some of them date back for years, but there are expiry dates and some of them hadn't expired yet. So we mixed old cans and new cans and got this. It's mixed-can casserole and it's a once-in-a-lifetime experience.'

'I bet it is.'

'And there was flour and cocoa and something called dehydrated eggs and sugar and we've made sort of a chocolate cake,' Karli told him.

'It's more a chocolate crunch,' Jenna said darkly with a warning glance at him. 'But it's something to put our candles on.'

'Candles?' He was feeling way out of frame.

'I told you. There were candles in the bottom drawer,' Karli said proudly. 'That's what made us remember it's my five and three-quarter'th birthday. I found them and said they looked like great

big birthday candles and Jenna said, ''Let's do it.''
Do you want to see?' She hauled open the door of
the refrigerator to show him.

The 'cake' stood in all its glory. It was as Jenna
had said, a sort of chocolate crunch—a layer of
brownish biscuity substance that covered the plate.
The candles were huge emergency household candles and they'd squeezed on five full candles, with
one that had been a quarter burnt in the centre.

'The three quarters for three quarter years is the
one in the middle,' Karli told him and he smiled.

'Hey, I figured that. Well done you.'

'Well done us,' Jenna said, and grinned. 'Eat, Mr
Jackson.'

'Can I have a beer?' he said faintly, and Karli
sighed in five-and-three-quarter-year-old exasperation.

'Beer's horrid.'

'Beer's essential.'

'I took it all out of the fridge,' she told him. 'It
was really hard to get the cake in. I packed it into
the cupboard but Jenna found it and made me put
some back.'

'Thank you, Jenna,' he told her, and he smiled
at her across the table.

She smiled back.

Whoa. What was happening here?

She was just smiling—but what a smile!

He rose to get a beer. Fast. Because it wasn't the beer he wanted. He wanted to break whatever was happening between the two of them.

This was really dumb. This woman was from a way of life that had nothing to do with him. She was here for another two nights and she'd be gone.

She had no business smiling at him like this.

He took a long time to get his beer, to open it and to sit back down at the table, and when he did he had himself under control again.

Almost.

Almost wasn't enough.

He worried her.

Jenna had far too much to be worried about to add Riley Jackson to her list, but still he worried her. He sat across the table and ate his casserole with evident enjoyment, but every move he made spoke of almost indescribable weariness.

He filled the room with his presence. His smile was magnetic and his gentleness with Karli was wonderful. He was a man who should be in a comfy home with a wife and children who loved him to bits. Instead of which he was here. Looking like this.

His face shocked her. The moment she'd seen him as she'd come out of the shower, it had been all she could do not to exclaim in dismay. His face was almost grey with fatigue and his eyes were bloodshot and exhausted. Had he worked solidly for the last two days? By the look of him he'd worked every waking minute, and there'd been far too few sleeping minutes.

He should be in bed right now, she thought. But at least she could feed him. The cake was probably dreadful, but the casserole had turned out okay and he looked as if he was relishing every mouthful.

'There's more on the stove,' she told him and he looked up and grinned and her heart did this silly little sideways skip.

'There won't be more for long,' he told her.

'Don't you eat while you're out working?'

'I have my beans.'

'Yeah? You've eaten beans for two days straight?'

'I can do it for a fortnight before I risk scurvy.'

'But why would you want to?'

'There's work to be done and only me to do it,' he said briefly before he re-addressed himself to the casserole.

It didn't make sense. The man had to have money. Where had the plane come from?

'The plane's yours?' she said tentatively and he looked up again, surprised.

'Yes, ma'am.'

'Then…why don't you sell the plane and live somewhere a bit closer to civilisation?'

'This is civilisation.' Another grin, though the weariness was so embedded that his grin was a bit lopsided. 'Actually…' he motioned round the room '…this is amazingly civilised. How did you do it? How did you stop the dust getting in?'

'Newspapers,' Karli volunteered between mouthfuls. 'Lots and lots of newspapers.'

'Newspapers?'

'It was all we could find,' Jenna told him. 'If you want to stop the dust permanently you'll have to do some carpentry. But meanwhile we've used newspaper to stuff chinks in the weatherboards and fill the cracks. We attacked one of the falling-down sheds for spare boards. We nailed boards over broken windows. We stuffed the gaps with more newspapers. I hope you've finished with last week's news,' she told him. 'If you haven't, it's a bit of a traipse around the house from page to page.'

He managed to smile again, but he looked dumbfounded. 'There wasn't much in the newspapers,' he managed. 'We lost the cricket.'

There was a long pause while he concentrated on eating for a bit, and then he stared across at her again. He looked down to Karli, who was tracing the cracks on her ancient china plate with her fork, and then he looked back to Jenna.

'I can't believe you've worked so hard.'

'I believe you've worked hard yourself,' she told him. She shouldn't worry, she thought. But she worried. He looked so exhausted.

'But I'm not Nicole Razor's child,' Riley said and she stilled. Sympathy did a fast exit, stage left.

'What's that supposed to mean?'

'Your parents are Nicole Razor and Charles Svenson. There's money to burn in those circles. I can't imagine that you've ever needed to do a day's work in your life.'

Here it was again. The prejudice that followed her everywhere.

'I work,' she snapped.

'You don't need to.'

'Of course I need to. How else can I live?'

'But you're wealthy. You offered to pay for a plane ride to Adelaide.'

'That's because I was desperate,' she told him. 'I'd have paid with plastic and then spent years paying it off.'

'I don't believe you.'

'You spend a whole bunch of time not believing me,' she snapped, rising and carrying the plates to the sink. Carefully turning her back on him. 'It's getting to be a habit.'

Let it go, she told him under her breath. Leave it.

But he wasn't leaving it.

'If your father doesn't support you, what do you do for a living?'

'Is that any of your business?'

'No, but—'

'How do you support this place?' she demanded, trying desperately to turn the conversation. 'Have you got a marijuana crop on the side?'

He grinned at that. 'Sure. A whole green paddock of marijuana nodding gently in the breeze. Just step out through the manicured gardens, walk on down the avenue of oaks, smile at the farmhands tending the sheep and you'll see the first of my cultivated crops on the right.'

'See, you won't tell me,' she said, still with her back to him. 'So why should I tell you what I do for a living?'

'Jenna's a nurse,' Karli volunteered.

Silence. Then: 'Thank you, Karli,' Riley said gravely. 'What sort of a nurse?'

'She helps the doctors when they operate,' Karli told him. 'She works a lot and a lot. She keeps wanting to come and see me, but she can't 'cos it's too far and she doesn't get any days off in a row.'

'And where does Jenna live?' Riley asked and Jenna wheeled to face him.

'Butt out, Jackson. This is none of your business.'

But the conversation had her excluded.

'Jenna lives in a really cute little room,' Karli told him. 'It's up really high. We climb all these stairs and her window looks over roofs and chimneypots and there's a cat who comes in the window and purrs, only he's not Jenna's. He belongs to the landlady, but we like him. His name's Pudding. And Jenna has a bed with purple cushions all over it that we sewed together. Her sofa's next to the bed and that's where I sleep. It's really comfy and I like being next to Jenna. We make toast and we drink cocoa and we let Pudding the cat in and I like it.' Her voice was suddenly defiant, and the look that she gave Riley suggested that he might almost be threatening it.

'You like going there?'

'The lady at the school keeps asking that, 'cos Nicole says I should stay all the time at school, but the school lady asked me a lot of questions and then she said she can't see any need to ask Nicole's permission when Jenna's my sister.'

Riley's eyes flashed to Jenna. 'So you're not supposed to have Karli.'

'Of course I am,' Jenna snapped, thoroughly disconcerted. He was finding out too much about her for comfort. Somehow she had to put a stopper on Karli's tongue—but the fact that Karli was talking was a joy in itself.

'We have a birthday cake to eat,' she reminded them, moving right on. 'Mr Jackson, will you light the candles?'

He cast her a doubtful glance, as if there were more questions he wanted to ask. But the cake was waiting. He lit the candles. He snuffed out the lantern and the only light was the ridiculously big candles on the cake.

'Sing ''Happy Birthday'',' Jenna ordered, and to her astonishment Riley stood and sang. He had a lovely voice, deep and rumbly and warm. He smiled across the cake at Karli as he sang and Jenna found it really hard to keep singing herself.

What was it with this man?

With 'Happy Birthday' finished, they solemnly clapped—five and three-quarter times (a sort of muffled thump for the three quarters) with an extra clap to make her grow—and then Karli blew her candles out in four big breaths.

'Every extra blow more than one means you have a boyfriend,' Jenna told her sister. 'That means you have three boyfriends.'

'Silly.' Karli chuckled in the dark, watching the last glow from the blown-out wicks disappear into darkness. 'The only boy here is Mr Jackson and he's too big for me. He can be your boyfriend,' she said generously and Jenna found herself blushing.

Oh, for heaven's sake.

She moved towards the lantern, guessing where it was in the dark, but Riley was before her. They reached the lantern at the same time and their hands touched.

And stayed touching.

'I'll light it,' Riley said, and was his voice just a trifle unsteady? 'I have the matches.'

'Good. Great.' Somehow she made herself draw back until the light flickered on and the room became normal again. Almost normal.

But Karli was staring at her sad excuse for a chocolate cake, made under the most primitive of conditions, and she was beaming as if she'd been given the world. 'This is the bestest birthday,' she whispered.

'I have a present for you,' Riley told her and he smiled and left the room.

'Jenna told me you couldn't get me a present because there aren't any shops,' Karli called as Jenna leaned back against the sink and tried to get her bearings.

'I don't need to go to the shops to get my present,' he called back, his voice muffled through the wall. There was the sound of much foraging and Karli started to look excited.

'What do you think it will be?'

'Maybe he's got you a cow,' Jenna suggested, intrigued herself. 'That'll put Pudding's nose out of joint.'

'Pudding wouldn't like a cow.'

'And a cow wouldn't fit in our suitcase on the way home.' She smiled and called out: 'Karli says she doesn't want a cow, Mr Jackson.'

'It's not a cow. I'm wrapping it up now.'

'I guess if he's wrapping it up it can't be a cow,' Jenna told Karli, and she watched as the little girl practically lit within with excitement.

She knew exactly how Karli would be feeling right now. In the past, birthdays for Karli would have been exactly the same as they'd been for Jenna. They'd either be forgotten completely or they'd be occasions to show off. They'd be huge, glittering affairs with jugglers and clowns and caterers and the children of every celebrity worth their salt, none of whom she knew, and parents drinking too much on the sidelines and gushing kisses and paparazzi...

Ugh.

There was still time, she thought. She could give Karli a happy childhood—if she was allowed to.

There was much thumping happening next door.

'I'm having trouble with my gift-wrapping,' Riley called. 'There seems to be a dearth of newspaper. Can I pull some out of the chinks?'

'You do and you're dead.'

'Not even for a birthday?'

'Not even for a birthday.'

Silence.

'Okay. Necessity is the mother of invention,' he announced. 'Close your eyes, Karli.'

Karli squeezed her eyes so shut her little nose was wrinkled to a quarter of its normal length. She was practically vibrating with anticipation.

Jenna was starting to do some anticipating herself. Her soap had been a sorry sort of offering, but it was the best she'd been able to do. The fact that it had been received with such delight had choked her up.

What would Riley produce?

Riley walked back into the room with his hands behind his back. He looked at the eyes-squeezed-shut Karli and he grinned. He looked across at Jenna and started to smile—and then thought better of it.

The tension zoomed back with a fierceness that took her breath away.

Concentrate on Karli, she told herself, and Riley had obviously decided that was the best thing to do, too.

'Are your eyes closed really, really tight?' he asked, and grinned as Karli nodded her head so hard one of her braids fell free.

He waited, drawing out the delicious anticipation for as long as he could. Then: 'Open now,' he told Karli and held out his hand.

Karli opened her eyes—and stared. Riley was holding out something long and black and a bit frayed around the edges.

'It's a sock.'

'Well guessed, Miss Karli.' Riley grinned still more. 'It is indeed a sock. It's my very best sock, however, specially laundered by the famous Maggie in honour of this auspicious occasion. I figured if Santa Claus can put Christmas presents in stockings, then I can put birthday presents in socks. Take it. It's yours. There's something inside.'

Karli stared across at Jenna, as if awaiting instructions, and Jenna smiled. 'Hold your breath while you check it out, Karli,' she advised. 'Men's socks smell.'

'Hey.' Riley sounded offended. 'You're casting aspersions on my Maggie.'

'Heaven forbid.'

He smiled at her, a gently laughing smile, and Jenna felt her heart twist again. He walked forward and laid the sock in Karli's lap—and then stepped back.

'Happy five and three-quarther'th birthday,' he told her.

Karli lifted the sock with caution, holding it out at full stretch by its top corner. Even from across the room Jenna could see it was heavy, weighed down by something large stuffed into the foot.

'What is it?' Karli breathed and held it to the light.

'Guess,' Riley told her.

She felt it with care, extending the moment for all it was worth.

'It feels like a rock.'

'You are too clever,' Riley told her, as if she'd just done something extraordinary. 'But what sort of a rock?'

A rock, Jenna thought blankly. She'd thought her soap was a sad effort. How could he pull off a rock?

A pet rock maybe? Was Karli young enough to be talked into enthusiasm for a pet rock?

Better than pet dust, she thought with wry humour. But not much.

'Pull it out,' Riley was advising, and Karli did, cautiously, as if it might bite.

It was a slab of rock, maybe four inches wide, eight inches long and two or three inches deep. It was soft gray and dusty, and jagged as if it had just been pulled out of the dirt. Karli slid it down onto the table and gazed at it in confusion.

'What is it?'

'What do you see?' Riley asked her gently and she looked perplexed. But then she frowned, concentrating, and Jenna leaned forward to see for herself.

There was an imprint on the rock's surface. It was a six-pointed star, with tiny round circles embedded along each of the star points.

'What does it look like?' Riley asked Karli, and the little girl traced the imprint with care.

'Like…a starfish?'

'Hey.' His smile was delighted. 'Exactly right. Now turn it over.'

She slid it over, moving slowly and with wonder, as if it just might turn out to be infinitely precious and she wasn't taking any chances. There on the other side was a shell, a mollusc, a beautifully coiled thing embedded deep into the rock.

'It's a shell,' she said, wondering.

'Not just a shell,' he told her. 'It's an amazingly special shell. And an amazingly special starfish.' He watched her finger tracing the shell with wonder. 'Karli, you know the dust you walked over on Thursday when you walked from the train platform?'

'Yes.'

'A million years ago that dust was sand at the bottom of a very big ocean. Once upon a time this place was all under water, and this starfish and this little sea-snail were crawling around the ocean floor, right where you're sitting.'

Her eyes flew up to Riley's. 'Really?'

'Really. You're sitting in the middle of an ocean, Karli. An ancient ocean that ceased to be an ocean a million years ago.'

She could hardly take it in, Jenna thought, watching the little girl's changing face. But she was trying.

'My starfish and my snail were alive a million years ago?'

'Yep,' he told her. 'And when they died they were buried on the ocean floor. Sand came up over them. The waves washed over them, over and over. Gradually the ocean disappeared, but still they stayed where they were buried. They stayed and they stayed, and the sand that buried them pressed down so hard that it became rock. Then this afternoon while I was digging out a pipe taking water to my cattle, this rock slipped up from under the ground. It was almost as if it had been waiting for a million years for this very special occasion. For Karli's five and three-quarter'th birthday.'

Jenna blinked. She found she had to blink several times.   Karli was gazing at Riley with stars in her eyes.

'And now it's mine?'

'It's yours to do with as you like, Karli,' he told her. 'If you like, when you get to a city you can take it to the museum and ask them to tell you exactly how old it is. You can look at the other rocks and see what else has been found from long ago. Sometimes museums really like rocks like this and maybe if it's very, very special they'll ask if they can borrow it and put it in a glass case so that everyone can see your special rock. If they do that then they'll put a notice on the bottom of the case saying where it was found and that it's your rock.

It's your very special birthday gift, Karli. Your starfish and your sea-snail.'

Karli turned to Jenna, her face glowing.

'My sea-snail. My starfish.'

'Yes.' She was having a bit of trouble with her voice.

'It's dirty,' she told Jenna. 'I'll be able to wash it with my new soap.'

'You can do that.'

'It's lovely.' Karli turned back to Riley. 'It's the bestest present. Now let's eat some cake.'

CHAPTER SIX

THE cake was not great. The cake, in fact, was ghastly, but Karli would have eaten cardboard if she'd been told it was birthday cake and Riley manfully got his down. Then, with the excitement over, Karli drooped and Jenna took her off to bed while Riley did the washing-up.

She came back into the kitchen as he was stacking newly washed plates on her newly washed shelves. He was fingering each plate as if he couldn't believe it.

She stood in the doorway for a moment and watched him. He was so big. His masculinity filled the room, she thought. And here he was, polishing his plates as if they were giving him pleasure. The man was seriously...nice?

He turned and found her watching, and she found herself starting to blush.

'What?' he demanded and she hesitated, searching for the answer. What? She didn't know what the question was. What?

'I like to see a man immersed in domesticity,' she told him at last, and she managed a smile.

'There's been little enough domesticity around here to make me notice it when I see it.'

'Hey, I'm domestic.'

'Would Maggie agree?'

'Sure she would.'

She knew nothing about him, she thought. Nothing. She was in his house, he was supplying their food and accommodating them and being wonderful to her little half-sister and she knew nothing about him at all.

'Where's Maggie?' she asked.

'At Munyering.'

'Where's Munyering?'

'Out the back of beyond,' he told her, and then, as she looked exasperated, he motioned south. 'It's about five hundred miles thataway.'

'So you and Maggie have a distant relationship.'

'About as close as I ever want with a woman,' he told her, and then looked as if he didn't understand why he'd just said what he'd said. He caught himself. 'I mean... We suit each other just fine.'

'But she's not your wife.'

'No.'

'You're definitely not married?'

'No.'

'Have you ever been married?'

'What is this?'

'Twenty questions,' she told him. 'You know far too much about me and I know nothing about you. Have you ever been married?'

'Once. It didn't work out.'

'Kids?'

'No.'

'Dogs? Guinea pigs? Budgerigars?'

'No and no and no.'

'Friends?'

'No.' That was out before he could stop it. He stilled and she met his eyes across the room and their gaze locked and held.

'No friends,' she said softly. 'Apart from Karli, who's your devoted friend for life. She's gone to sleep clutching her fossil like other kids go to bed clutching their teddy bear.'

'Why hasn't Karli got a teddy bear?'

The question came out of left field, turning the tables neatly.

'I imagine she's been given several,' she said slowly. 'Nicole would have lost them or given them away or simply left them behind in hotel rooms because they were a nuisance. She'd buy more on a whim. Then when she and Brian split, Brian would have replaced whatever Nicole supplied by something that would have annoyed the hell out of Nicole. And so on. I learned as a kid never to show affection for any of my toys. If my father gave it to me then my mother would destroy it and vice versa. In the end it was easier not to get attached at all.'

'So you were left with nothing?'

'I escaped,' she told him. 'We're talking about Karli.'

'How can you say you've escaped?' he said gently. 'You don't escape the past.'

'Says the man with no friends.' Two could play at turning the tables. 'I can't believe you have no friends. That's a crazy statement.'

'I don't exactly live in a place where friends drop in.'

'You don't live here, though, do you?' she said cautiously. 'I mean, not all the time. This is a place you come to work.'

'The place where I base myself is just as isolated.'

'But not as dusty.'

'No,' he admitted, smiling a little. 'Not as dusty. You really have done an amazing job.'

'It was fun.'

'I've never met a single woman who'd think this was fun,' he told her and she shrugged.

'You move in the wrong circles.'

'Unlike you. Child of rock star and racing driver.'

'They have nothing to do with me. My friends aren't their friends. My friends are mostly nurses and, yes, most of us know what hard work is and we know it can be a pleasure all by itself.'

He was staring at her as if he couldn't work her out.

'Are you really a nurse?'

'I really am a nurse.'

'How the hell does Charles Svenson's daughter end up being a nurse?'

'I don't think you understand anything about me,' she said softly.

'No. I don't. So tell me.' He left the sink and sat down, gesturing to the chair on the other side of the table.

'You're tired.' She hesitated, but sat down as well. 'You don't want to listen to my life history when you should be going to bed.'

'Sure I'm tired,' he said, and he threw her that gorgeous, disconcerting smile. 'I need a bedtime story.'

'I...'

'Just tell me,' he said gently, and suddenly his hand came across the table and gripped hers. Strong and sure and compelling. 'I want to know.'

'I don't know why,' she said, trying to haul her hand away, but still he held.

'I don't know either,' he admitted. 'But tell me. Tell me about your parents.'

'I don't... I don't know my parents. I never have.'

'Why not?'

She faltered. How to describe the relationship or the lack of the relationship? How to tell anyone?

But his hand was warm and strong and he'd given Karli a gift that Jenna knew she would treasure for ever.

She owed him the truth.

'Nicole gave birth to me, but that was it,' she told him, tugging once more on her fingers and then giving up. She liked her hand being in his, she decided. It didn't mean a thing, she knew—but she liked it.

'And your father?' he prodded and she made herself go on.

'Charles fathered me but there wasn't any attachment there either. I was the only link they had to each other. They hated each other and I was a financial obligation. I was placed in boarding-school when I was younger than Karli. Then they fought over who should pay—and who had to shoulder responsibility for me during the long holidays. Which of them had to fork out for hotel bills for me.'

'Hotel bills?'

'You don't think they'd care for me themselves, do you?'

'I guess not.'

She shrugged. 'I didn't mind the hotels so much. But school... Every now and then the school would ask that I be taken away as no one had paid the fees. The kids gave me a hard time about my celebrity parents who refused to pay and never came near me. Then, when I was fourteen, the school said I couldn't stay any longer. My fees were so far overdue that the school wrote to my parents and said to come and collect me.'

She hesitated, but she'd gone this far. She might as well tell him everything. 'So I lied and forged a letter from Nicole and told the school authorities I had to catch the train and meet my mother in London.'

He frowned. Still his hand held hers. 'Why did you lie?'

'Because no one was ever coming to get me,' she said, and the old anger echoed in her voice. 'Every girl in the school knew that my fees hadn't been paid. I hated it. I think... I hated everyone then. Anyway, I caught the train and went to

London and tried to get work. I lived on my wits for months until a reporter from a tabloid daily found me.'

Riley was rubbing her fingers, caressing each in turn. 'How did he find you?' he asked gently, and she flinched at the gentleness in his voice.

'Don't you dare feel sorry for me.'

His lips curved into a half-smile. 'I daren't.'

'I was fine,' she told him, almost belligerently. 'I had a job washing dishes in a little Chinese restaurant where they didn't ask any questions and they paid cash. Neither of my parents even knew I was missing. That was okay by me. But I was stupid enough to talk about my background to one of the kids in the squat I was living in and he told the press what Nicole Razor's daughter was doing. For money. The press had a field-day.'

'Tough,' Riley said softly, and she flashed a suspicious glance at him. But his face was almost impersonal. That was how she needed him to be, and somehow he knew it.

'So what happened then?' he asked, and she made herself continue.

'My parents were mortified. Of course. Their daughter living as a street kid. But they weren't as mortified as I was. I was dragged back to school by one of my father's employees. My mother's agent rang me and told me I was ruining Nicole's career and I should be ashamed. I had to put up with the girls at school reading the whole story in the scandal pages of the newspapers.' She shrugged and managed a small smile. 'Okay, you can feel sorry for me now a little bit, if you like.'

He smiled back, just a little. 'How much can I feel sorry for you?'

'Minimum,' she told him. 'I don't need it. I didn't need it then.'

'Why not?'

She grinned. 'Because from then on it was better. It was like I'd hit a wall and managed to get through. I'd learned some street smarts and the bullies at school learned to leave me alone.'

'I might have guessed they would,' he said, and there was no mistaking the sudden admiration in his voice. 'Any woman who conquers my roofing iron must have run rings around a few school bullies.'

'I did,' she said, and her smile deepened. This man had the capacity to lighten her spirits. Lighten her…life?

'So then what?' he prodded, and she had to force herself to remember where she was in her pathetic little story.

'I'd had enough,' she told him. 'I stayed at school until I was old enough to get into a nursing course, and then I was out of there so fast you couldn't see me for dust. I didn't talk about my parents and they sure as heck didn't talk about— or to—me. I worked my way through my nursing training and I've asked for and accepted no help from either of my parents since. That's it. End of story. If it wasn't for me finding out—via the tabloids again—about Karli's existence, I'd have had no contact with them since.'

Silence.

It had been a long speech for Jenna, she decided as she sat still with her hand still in his. She'd so seldom talked about her life. Just once, as a lonely fourteen-year-old, she'd told someone the story of her upbringing. She'd thought the kid in the squat was a friend and he'd sold her story for money.

She'd learned the hard way to shut up.

Riley could sell this story for money, too, she knew. The tabloids would have a field-day with what was happening, especially now with Nicole recently dead.

She looked across the table, absorbing the fact that he was still holding her hand and he didn't look as if he intended to give it up.

'I…you won't tell? I mean, it's private. I don't…'

'Do you really think I'd sell you out?'

She blinked. Riley was looking at her as if he couldn't believe what he was seeing. But the expression on his face…

She could trust this man. She knew she could trust him.

'You really are on your own,' he said slowly, but she shook her head.

'I'm twenty-six. I have a career, and back home I have friends. I'm not alone any more. It's only Karli who's desperately alone. Nicole's dead, but Karli's still legally dependent on Brian. I don't know what will happen to her now.'

His eyes were on hers, asking questions. Receiving answers? Maybe. He could see into her, this man. The more she saw of him, the more she knew she was exposed.

He was still holding her hand.

'You'll try and keep her with you,' he said softly, as if he was stating the obvious, and she nodded.

'Yes.'

'And who'll pay?'

But it was a mistake. She'd been telling all, he'd been pushing the boundaries and suddenly here was a boundary she didn't want broached.

'Back off,' she said, and her anger startled her as well as him. But it was the way to go. In truth she had no answer to his question and she'd learned—the hard way—that in times of crisis it was infinitely better to attack rather than defend. She hauled her hand away from his and stared at him across the table—to see him looking astonished.

'Hey, I'm not about to push. If you don't want to talk about it, that's fine by me.'

He looked taken aback.

Maybe she had overreacted.

'Um…whoops.' She gave a rueful grin, but she kept her hand very firmly on her side of the table. 'Sorry. It's just I'm not used to people helping. I'm not used to people asking questions when they don't want something of me.'

'I don't want anything of you.'

'I know that.' She did.

'You really are by yourself.'

'No,' she said, and, despite her regret at her reaction, the anger was still there, try as she would to fight it. 'Alone I can cope with. I've learned that alone is a really good way to be. But now I have Karli and it's a whole new world. Somehow I have to figure out a way to keep her safe. If she'd been left money…'

'But Brian's robbed her of that.'

'As you say.' Her face closed. It was time to move on. For heaven's sake, what was she thinking of, telling her personal problems to this man? Just because he was big and kindly and he'd given a gift to Karli that had made her want to weep...

He was exhausted. She could see it in his face— and she was none too perky herself. She'd worked very, very hard today.

'It's time we went to bed,' she said, attempting briskness. 'I'm sorry about the life-story bit.'

'I asked.'

'Yeah, people do,' she told him. 'And I'm usually not stupid enough to answer.'

'I don't think you're stupid.'

There was a moment's silence. A loaded silence. She stared down at her hand that had so recently lain in his. She missed the contact. The warmth. The strength.

She had to be sensible. She needed to be sensible.

'You'll go out again in the morning?'

'I have more work to do.'

'Us, too. We thought we'd attack the bedrooms in the morning.'

'There's no need.'

'Call it payment for board and lodging. There's only one more day before the train comes through and Karli and I are having fun.'

'Fun?'

'Yeah, it is.' She smiled, moving on. 'We're enjoying ourselves. And…it's time out before we face what we have to face.'

'You know you'll have paparazzi all over you the minute you get on that train.'

She stilled. 'Pardon?'

'They know you're here.'

'The press knows I'm here?'

'I was talking to the Territory police today and there's huge press interest. You could sell your story—'

He got no further. She was standing, her face blazing anger. 'You told them. You radioed them and told them I was here. So I'll have every newspaper reporter and every cameraman known to man in Karli's face the minute I get on board that train. You toe-rag. You low-life, belly-crawling worm. You lying, cheating, dirt-bag.'

'Hey, steady on,' he said mildly, but she was in full swing.

'How much did they pay you? How much have you embellished the story? And are you going to head out to your radio right now and add in what

I've just told you for good measure? I thought I could trust you, Riley Jackson. I'm stupid, stupid, stupid. Of all the two-timing, low-down, bottom-feeding—'

'You don't feel you might just be being a teensy bit overdramatic?'

She paused for breath. The man was looking amused. Amused!

'Dramatic?' She grabbed the first thing to hand—the remains of one sad chocolate cake—and threw it straight at him. It hit him fair in the chest. It rolled to the floor.

It bounced.

His lips quirked.

'If you laugh I'm going to have to kill you,' she said carefully and his lips quirked again.

'Death by chocolate cake. I can see that.'

'It's nothing to laugh about.'

'No, but it's nothing to yell about either.' He rose and retrieved the cake. 'We ate some of this,' he said, examining it doubtfully from all angles. 'It looks like it's turning to concrete. What do you reckon it'll do to our insides?'

'It's a fine chocolate cake,' she snapped, and the quirk of his lips turned into full-scale laughter.

'Dehydrated eggs, no butter and flour milled last century…' He lifted it up to the light and examined it some more before dropping it into the waste bucket—where it definitely bounced again. 'It's a fine chocolate cake,' he agreed, still grinning. 'Or a fine small nuclear missile, ready charged.'

She swallowed. 'Do you mind? And stop changing the subject. I was in—'

'Yeah. You were in the middle of calling me a low-life, belly-crawling maw-worm or some such.' His tone was suddenly admiring. 'You've been practising your insults. They're very good.'

'Luckily,' she said scathingly, 'I've had heaps of people to practise on.'

'I guess you have,' he said thoughtfully. 'Nicole, Charles, Brian. The kid who sold your story to the papers. Others maybe. Jenna, I'm not like that.'

'You told—'

'I didn't tell,' he said, and the restraint in his voice was suddenly obvious. It was as if he were trying to placate a child. 'You know the lady who was reading Karli a story when Brian came into the carriage to tell you that Nicole was dead?'

It was so unexpected a statement that it caught her flat-footed. She stared. 'What's that got to do with it?'

'Will you listen?' he said patiently. 'It seems the lady wasn't just any little old lady. Enid's a chief magistrate of the West Australian court, retired.

She's one very astute woman and she wanted to know what happened to you.'

'But—'

'So Enid made enquiries,' Riley said patiently. 'As the train continued and she didn't see you again she got more and more worried. By the time the train reached Kalgoorlie she'd instigated a search. When you weren't on the train she forced the rail authorities to contact the police. Brian had to face a very uncomfortable interview, and then the police started searching the track. They contacted a couple of the people who collected goods from the train when it stopped here. One of the locals remembered I was staying here. He radioed me and I let the police know your whereabouts. After Enid's fuss, if I hadn't confirmed you were here you'd have had search parties out looking for you, planes doing overhead searches—the works.'

It stopped her in full flight. It shocked her to silence. She stood and stared.

'So…we wouldn't have died at the siding.'

'You'd have had a bad twenty-four hours, but Enid would have got you help.'

'I… I don't know what to say.'

He grinned again. 'Try an insult. I really like your insults.'

'Shut up,' she told him and his grin broadened.

'You can do better than that.'

She glared and he grinned some more.

'Hey, you accused me of telling the press. I've explained it wasn't me. It's me who's supposed to be glaring.'

So why was she glaring? It was because he was smiling, she thought. It was because…she had no defences. She just had to look at this man and things inside her crumpled that had no business crumpling. She made a desperate attempt to haul herself together.

'I'm sorry,' she managed.

'Think nothing of it,' he said, his tone almost avuncular. 'I enjoyed it. No one's ever called me a low-life, belly-crawling worm before.'

'I can't think why not,' she said, and he grinned again.

'Ouch.'

His tiredness had receded, she thought suddenly. The fatigue that seemed almost part of the man had faded a little. She'd made him laugh.

She liked it that she'd made him laugh.

Oh, for heaven's sake, this was dangerous territory and she had no business treading there. She needed to move on.

She needed to concentrate on Karli.

'So... So you've told everyone that I'm here?' she managed and his smile faded.

'No. I told the Territory police. But the officer I talked to said there was huge press interest. They searched the train at Kalgoorlie, which created interest. Other passengers saw what happened and they've figured out who you are. The police sergeant said the press won't be told exactly where you are, but everyone knows you got off the train somewhere along here. So if I was a reporter, I'd be waiting for you to get back on the train again.'

She stared up at him, immeasurably distressed, but there was no reassurance in his face. Riley was telling the truth. He didn't like it any more than she did, she thought suddenly. And at least...at least the eyes she was looking into were totally frank.

How could she have called him those names?

Riley Jackson was a man she could trust. Among all the fear and disillusion of the last few days—of her whole life, if she was honest—this stood out as an absolute truth. Whatever else Riley was, he was a man who was ruthlessly honest.

Riley's honesty didn't make what he was telling her one bit more palatable. She bit her lip.

'Which means Karli...'

'Karli will face cameras and reporters as soon as you board.'

'Which will be awful,' she said. 'It's the last thing she needs. I never should have got off.'

'If Brian's as bad as he sounds, you hardly had a choice.'

'At least I won't have to have anything to do with him again,' she whispered, thinking it through. 'If Karli had inherited, then Brian would want her. This way, he thinks he's won and he'll go away with the money and leave us alone.'

Riley stayed silent.

'But what will I do?'

'Get back on the train,' he suggested. 'Face the music. Shield Karli as much as you can, but explain to her that there'll be couple of awful days before you get on with the rest of your life. Hit Perth in a blaze of publicity and make life very, very unpleasant for Brian.'

'Why?'

'Because he deserves it,' he said flatly. 'For all Brian knows, you're dead of thirst by now. If Enid hadn't contacted the police there'd have been no search party, no enquiries, nothing.'

'He mustn't realise…'

'He'll have realised. Either that or the man's a fool.'

Jenna swallowed. No. Brian wasn't a fool. And this was his daughter he'd put at risk.

She could bring him down, she thought. She could denounce him to the gutter press and they'd have a field-day. But…

'He's Karli's father,' she whispered. 'What sort of legacy does that leave her?' She gazed at him for a long minute, searching for answers.

There were none.

'If you'll excuse me,' she faltered. 'I need to go to bed.'

'To face unpleasant facts in the morning?'

She shrugged. 'They might seem less hopeless then,' she admitted.

'Jenna…'

Riley stood looking down at her in the flickering lamplight. What was it with this man? Jenna felt small and lonely and utterly bereft—sensations she hadn't felt since childhood. She'd decided early on that feeling small and lonely and bereft wasn't the way to survive. She'd learned tough.

So where was tough when she needed it most? She needed tough right now.

And when his hands came out and caught hers in a gesture that seemed almost unconscious, she felt the tough layer she'd so carefully built up slip away even further. He made her feel… He made her feel…

She didn't know how he made her feel. Just different. Alive. And very, very vulnerable.

Something of how she was feeling must have got through to the man before her. He was a fool if he couldn't see how confused she was—and if there was one thing she'd learned by now it was that Riley Jackson was no fool.

'It'll seem better in the morning,' he told her and there was something in his voice that told her he was as unsure as she was. He was entering unchartered territory as well. The territory of caring. 'You'll get through this.'

'I know I will,' she whispered. 'I always have. But I don't see how I can shield Karli.'

His hold on her hands tightened. He stood staring down at her, his mouth twisting into an expression that Jenna couldn't define. She looked up into his eyes—and then she looked away. She didn't trust…herself?

He was so close. So strong. So… So Riley. She stood in her bare feet with her soft pastel dress seeming somehow too insubstantial. It was no barrier. Not when she wanted to sink against him. To feel his strength. To have him hold her.

He was so close to her heart.

The silence went on and on. Absolute silence. The world stopped.

And something within Jenna's heart formed and grew—bud to flower almost instantaneously. It grew so fast that it threatened to overwhelm her.

What was it? Need? Desire?

Whatever it was, her overwhelming compulsion was to lay her head against this man's chest and claim it as her home. The home she'd never had was suddenly right here.

Right here in this man's heart.

Only it wasn't. Of course it wasn't. This man had nothing to do with her. He was a stranger. He was an Australian dust farmer of whom she knew nothing, except that he lived in the most barren place in the earth and he wanted nothing to do with any woman.

But he was holding her. And she was feeling...what? What was this sensation that was swelling beneath her breast, so much that she thought she must surely burst? Or cry. Or do something even more stupid, like falling against him and holding him hard against her and raising her face to his and...

No!

Somehow she made herself push away, so that Riley was holding her at arm's length, his face grave and troubled, and the weariness in his eyes replaced by concern.

'I'm sorry,' she managed. 'You have enough troubles of your own without landing you with mine.'

'Maybe I can help.'

'You already have. But from now on I'm on my own. Mr Jackson…'

'Riley.'

'Riley, then,' she whispered, and the word sounded wrong on her lips. It was as if it were the embrace she so desperately wanted to give him. Wanted him to give her.

'What's your biggest worry?'

'Karli,' she admitted. 'To make her face reporters. If there's media on the train and we're stuck on board for two days…'

'I can fly you out of here.'

'You said you couldn't.'

'I said I couldn't immediately,' he told her. 'Which was true. My job here is to get the bores operational and to make the house habitable enough for a couple of men to use as a base for muster.'

'Muster?'

'We'll bring in trucks and take the surviving herd south where they can graze on some decent feed. These poor beasts won't know themselves. But getting men to stay here before the place was liveable was impossible. You've saved me a couple of days' work. I've fixed the most urgent water problems. If I spend tomorrow making your repairs permanent—putting wood where you've stuffed newspapers—and spend another day south of here doing a head count, then I can fly out. That makes it Tuesday. You're welcome to come with me.'

'But...where will you go?' She gave a futile tug to her hands.

'Munyering. My home farm.'

'Another farm?' She forced her emotions to one side—sort of—and made herself concentrate. 'Like this one?'

He smiled at that. 'No, Jenna, not like this one. Munyering's isolated, but we have decent bore water and it's in much better condition.'

It'd have to be, she thought, but it was hard to think it. Hard to think anything, really, with this man's hands holding hers.

'Then...how could I reach civilisation from Munyering?'

'I'll take you.' And his fingers moved through hers in a gesture of reassurance.

It was strange, Jenna thought desperately. Riley was talking—he was touching her—as if he was unaware of the effect he was having. As if he didn't feel what was running through her hands. It was like an electric current, bringing warmth and strength and…'

And nothing. Make yourself think, she told herself harshly. Cut it out with the hormones. Just because this guy makes you feel like you want to jump him…

Jump him? What was she thinking?

She knew exactly what she was thinking.

'I'll refuel at Munyering and fly you on down to Adelaide,' he was saying. 'You can take a flight from there to wherever you want to go.'

Where did she want to go?

Home is where the heart is. The saying drifted through her mind with awful bleakness. According to that criterion she'd never had a home. Somehow she had to create one for Karli.

But at least she had a start. Riley would save them from the train. He'd fly them to Adelaide and then…

She looked up into his concerned face and felt her foundations shift.

This was crazy. What on earth was she thinking?

With a gasp she jerked her hands back and this time she was released. She stepped back as though fending him off, but Riley didn't follow.

'I'll pay you.'

'You'll do nothing of the kind.'

'I don't accept help without payment.'

'Then learn to do so. If not for you, then for Karli.'

'But you can't afford—'

'I can afford. Believe me, Jenna. Just accept.'

She sighed. It was all too hard. She didn't want to be beholden to this man. Not like this. But it seemed she had no choice.

She wasn't on her own any longer. Choices were out of her control. She had to think of Karli.

'I…thank you,' she whispered.

'Think nothing of it,' he said gently. 'And you don't need to thank me. You and Karli have worked long and hard making this place liveable. It's me who's grateful and I pay my debts.'

He was grateful? He was offering to fly them out of here because he felt grateful? Was that the emotion she wanted him to feel?

No. Not one bit.

'Go to bed, Jenna,' Riley said softly. 'You've done a hard two days' work.'

'So have you. Saving your cattle.'

'While you saved my house.' He stared around again as if he still couldn't believe what he was seeing. 'I'm aching to see it in the morning.'

'If it's still standing,' she said and she heard a note of asperity enter her voice. She couldn't help it. Was the man totally insensitive? Here she was practically aching for him to touch her—kiss her senseless and make her forget every darned thing she'd ever taught herself about keeping her distance—and he was talking about housekeeping.

She glared up at him, aware that it was crazy to glare, but she couldn't help herself.

He gazed back at her and his expression was inscrutable.

Then, finally, Riley touched her cheek lightly, as if he was touching something that was almost infinitely precious—and totally beyond his reach.

'It's late,' he said flatly, and his voice was solid and uncompromising. 'Go to bed, Jenna.'

Her glare faltered. Her hand lifted and caught his. Her eyes held his for a long moment. Asking questions she knew he couldn't answer.

Go to bed?

She had to. She must.

A girl had some dignity.

She dropped his hand as if it burned—then turned and fled before she did something she might regret for the rest of her life.

Maybe.

For a long time after Jenna left, Riley didn't stir from the kitchen. He sat over a can of beer—and then another and then another. He was weary beyond belief, but there was an inertia hanging over him that wouldn't let him move.

Or was it inertia? Maybe it was the unbearable thought of going out to the veranda and walking past the place where Jenna lay.

She was so beautiful. So lovely. A slip of a girl who'd fought her way in life, who reacted like a terrier who'd defend herself and her own to the death. He thought of what she'd faced as a kid, on the streets of London, fighting for a living, and he thought of her parents' privileged backgrounds, and he felt an anger surging through him that was almost overwhelming. No wonder she was prepared to fight for Karli's future. If she felt about Karli as he felt about her...

What sort of low-lifes were these people? Brian? Charles? The dead Nicole?

They needed to be shot, he thought, and then he remembered Nicole was already dead and caught himself in a half-smile. Maybe not. But damn, if he hadn't been here to help... He found himself squeezing his beer can so hard it crushed beneath his fingers. He stared down at the mangled metal in confusion.

'What the hell has this mess got to do with you, Riley Jackson?' he demanded of himself. 'You don't get involved. Remember? You know what you should do? Get in the plane and take the pair of them to Adelaide tomorrow. You've got the worst of the bore problems solved. You could take them and come back—it'd be only an extra day. So do it. Get rid of them fast. Get rid of trouble.'

Trouble.

The word drifted round and round the kitchen.

If he took them now he'd have to come back, he acknowledged, looking round the gleaming little kitchen with eyes that saw just how much work the pair of them had put in to get it the way it was. And, strangely, that was the problem. Take them to Adelaide and come back here? The thought was unbearable.

Why?

'What on earth are the pair of them doing to you?' Riley demanded. He lifted one of Karli's make-do birthday candles and stared at its dead wick as if it might give him answers. 'They're making you feel like you swore you'd never feel again.'

'I've never felt like this before.'

'Yeah, but you know what you're feeling, boy. Desire. Pure and simple.'

And yet it wasn't. He knew it wasn't. The vision of Jenna floated before him, and although Riley's hand clenched hard on his candle he knew it wasn't just lust that was making him feel this way. It was so much more.

It was the overwhelming need to make Jenna smile. To take the look of distrust from her eyes. To make Karli chuckle. To take away the hurt...

'Stop it right now!' He hurled the can savagely across the kitchen—and then, thinking better of it as it lay untidily on the newly scrubbed floor, he rose, retrieved it and carefully placed it in the waste. It lay on top of the remains of the chocolate cake.

It was a crazy chocolate cake. It had been one crazy birthday.

It had been wonderful.

'They're getting to you,' he told himself savagely. 'Watch out. If you're not careful you'll be caught up in the whole damned web again.'

He took a deep breath, steadying, then walked through the darkened house to the veranda.

Jenna was already in bed. There were two humps in the big bed, Jenna's body curved protectively around the child beside her.

Was she asleep? He wasn't sure. Her sheet moved almost imperceptibly in the moonlight with her deep, even breathing.

He wanted her. The ache was a fierce physical pain that threatened to overwhelm him. He could just walk forward to say goodnight, lean over, lift the sheet and kiss…

He did no such thing.

Instead he swore savagely under his breath, then walked back into his newly cleaned sitting room and threw himself onto the old settee. There was no way he could sleep on the veranda. Not feeling how he was feeling.

He'd do the house maintenance tomorrow and then he'd get the hell out of here. Back to his bores. Outback, where the only thing to concentrate on was sheer hard work.

Where a man could forget about women.

She heard him go.

She knew what he was doing. He didn't want to sleep on the veranda.

She knew how he was feeling.

She turned on her side and stared out into the starlit sky and tried to think why life had suddenly become more bleak.

Why life had suddenly become desperate.

CHAPTER SEVEN

'JENNA, Mr Jackson's hammering.'

Jenna surfaced with reluctance. It had been hours before she'd slept the night before, finally falling into uneasy slumber some time before dawn, but Karli was bouncing beside her, big with news.

'He's working and working and we should be up and helping him.'

Jenna groaned. Karli was immediately concerned.

'Are you sick?'

'No. I'm tired.'

'How can you be tired? We've slept for hours.'

'Hours.' She rolled over to check her watch and she landed on a rock. 'Ouch!'

'My fossil. Don't bend my starfish.'

'Your starfish bent me.'

There was no sympathy from Karli. 'We should get up and help Mr Jackson.'

'You help Mr Jackson.'

'I will,' Karli announced. 'You look after my starfish.'

*   *   *

It wasn't yet seven o'clock. By rights Jenna should disappear back into sleep. But the hammering continued. She heard it pause as Karli obviously approached. There was an intense conversation, a few giggles and then the hammering resumed. Only now there were two hammers.

Hammering before seven o'clock was surely against union rules. Where was a union when she needed one?

But sleeping with a rocky starfish was losing its attraction. If she only had two more days with Riley Jackson…well, she was darned if she was wasting them by sleeping with a rock.

They were outside. All she had to do was follow the sound of the childish questions, the low, gruff answers and the rhythmic hammering. He had her intrigued. He was so good to Karli. She slowed as she approached, listening in.

'Will we fly in your aeroplane?'

'Yes.'

'To your other house?'

'Yes.'

'Is your other house as horrible as this one?'

Jenna winced, but Riley chuckled.

'It's different.'

'Does it have as much dust?'

'We have much nicer dust at Munyering. And Maggie is a dust fixer, just like Jenna is a dust fixer. They're very similar women.'

'Is Maggie nice?'

'She's very nice.'

'Jenna's nice, too. Do you think Jenna's nice?'

Did she imagine it or was there a moment's hesitation. And then a certain amount of wariness. 'She's very nice.'

'She's not always dusty.'

'I can see that.' The laughter was back in Riley's voice.

Enough. Eavesdroppers heard no good of themselves and she was playing with fire. She ducked under a makeshift clothesline where six shirts and assorted socks and jocks were flapping in the wind. They were already dry. Laundry day on the farm?

They didn't see her approach and for a moment Jenna stood among the laundry and watched them. Riley had ceased hammering. He was sawing ancient weatherboards to size. Karli was sitting in the dust in her nightgown, banging a board onto the house with a nail as big as her hand and a hammer that was huge. She was concentrating absolutely and the nail was going in true.

And Riley was stripped to the waist, his broad chest was glistening with sweat as he sawed, and he looked…he looked…

Like the sort of guy you should run a mile from, she thought. An outback hero in a romance novel of the bodice-ripper variety. Toe-curlingly gorgeous.

Her toes were definitely curling.

He looked up from his work, he saw her and he grinned.

'Well, well. Sleeping Beauty rises. Karli and I decided you may well snooze for another hundred years.'

'There's something not very companionable about a rock,' she told him. 'Which is all Karli left me to sleep with. And might I remind you that it's not yet seven o'clock. Aren't there rules about industrial noise in residential areas before seven?'

'Is it almost seven?' he demanded. 'Heck. Almost lunch time.'

'What time did you wake?'

'Five.'

'So you've done your laundry.'

'Well noticed.'

'Won't Maggie do it for you?'

'Yep, but I'm fresh out of clean shirts and I need to keep myself nice for Miss Karli here.'

'They're hardly whiter than white,' she said, eying them with caution. 'Don't they dry hard in this water?'

'We outback men are tough,' he told her and grinned—and the bodice-ripper image intensified. So did the toe-curling.

Drat the man.

Riley handed a weatherboard to Karli, then squatted down and helped her fit it. Together they nailed. He was treating the child as if she were really a help, Jenna thought, and, damn, here came that stupid lump in her throat that was never far away when this man was close. Why?

She knew why.

With the weatherboard fitted, Riley rose and surveyed his handiwork. 'Enough,' he told Karli. 'It's time for lunch.'

'We haven't had breakfast yet.'

'How about brunch as an alternative?' He grinned. 'Seeing I've declared this as a day of domesticity I've even managed time to cook. I lay in my cot last night and thought: these two visitors from the old country have obviously categorised me as a rotten housekeeper so the best thing I can do is to show them I'm not a total wuss.'

Which was so far from what Jenna was thinking of him that she blinked.

'You mean you've actually managed to heat your baked beans?' she managed, and his smile widened.

'Nope. At great personal sacrifice I'm forgoing baked beans this morning. It's pancakes. I've already made the batter. Let's go.' He took Karli's hand and they started walking toward the back door. Jenna was left with no choice but to follow them, which she did, feeling like a small, obedient pup. A stunned pup.

'What do you mean, pancakes?' she asked his retreating back.

'Don't they have pancakes in England? Surely it's not all black pudding and spotted dick?'

'Well, yes. But...'

'Trust me, lady.' Riley ushered Karli through the back door, and then stood aside for Jenna to precede him. She walked past and her skin brushed his. She was wearing a halter top and shorts. Not enough of her skin was covered. Not enough of his skin was covered.

Did he have any idea of the effect he had on her? Trust him? He had to be joking.

Luckily Riley didn't notice her discomposure—or if he did he ignored it. Jenna had time to find her composure, sit herself down at the table with Karli and school her features into something akin to polite interest.

Polite interest, she told herself desperately. That was all she was allowed to feel.

Impossible ask.

'I like pancakes,' Karli announced. 'Can you really cook them?'

'You'd better believe it.'

They had no choice but to believe. While they watched in wonder, Riley poured batter into a hot pan, swirled, flipped and then flicked the finished product onto waiting plates.

'You've done this hundreds of times,' Jenna accused, and if her voice wasn't quite normal it was close enough. She hoped.

'Just as well for you guys,' Riley admitted. 'I make them with powdered milk, so they're one of the few foods that cooks up well out here. Mind, I had to scrape my first attempts off the ceiling.' He grinned. 'I got a bit ambitious with my flipping to start with. Okay. Hop in. There's a tin of jam in the crate behind you.'

'A tin?'

'You were expecting home-cooked preserves?' Another pancake flipped onto the pile and he sat down, cooking finished. 'The only thing to preserve here would be saltbush, and I don't fancy saltbush jam.'

'Ugh.'

'My sentiments exactly.'

'How can you make pancakes without egg?' Jenna was glaring as though suspecting him of some conjuring act.

'Powdered egg,' he told her briefly. He gave her a smug smile. 'It works better for pancakes than for chocolate cake—but you have to be a very experienced cook to know that. Now stop asking questions and eat.'

Jenna glared again, but Riley was ignoring her and concentrating on the important things in life. Pancakes. So was Karli. There was nothing for Jenna to do but concentrate as well.

The pancakes didn't just look delicious. They were delicious. Or maybe it was just the sensation of sitting at the table with this enigmatic man of whom Jenna knew nothing.

She did know nothing, she reminded herself desperately. It was silly to feel as she was feeling.

But as he teased Karli, as they discussed how much jam one pancake could hold, as they giggled like two five-year-olds and Karli blossomed into the laughing, happy little girl Jenna knew she could be, all she knew was that she was falling deeper in love by the minute.

That was what could be described as delicious, she acknowledged. Delicious, exhilarating—and altogether too stupid for words!

'Who taught you to cook pancakes?' Jenna asked as she surfaced for air three pancakes later. Karli had disappeared back to her hammer and nails—her newfound love of carpentry was far too important to be delayed by something as dull as food.

Jenna had been intent on scraping up a last morsel of jam as she asked. There was no immediate answer. She looked up and found Riley's face was suddenly grim. 'I said no more questions.'

'Until I ate my pancakes. If I eat one more I'll pop. So tell me. Your mum?'

'Not likely.'

The words were said harshly, and Jenna looked curiously across the table at Riley.

'That sounds like your childhood might have shades of mine,' she told him. 'Did it?'

'What do you mean?'

'You know what I mean.' She hesitated—but then, what had she to lose? Riley's good opinion? In a few days she'd be nothing but a memory to this man, she thought. She might as well be a pesky memory.

'The nurses I work with… The patients I care for…' she continued, watching his face. 'I can usually tell who's come from a happy background. I used to be incredibly jealous of kids whose parents loved them, so much so that it got to be a bit of a masochistic habit—choosing the people with a happy family.' She hesitated. 'I'm willing to bet your parents weren't into happy families.'

'That's none of your business.'

Jenna shrugged and started clearing. 'It's just...you seem to know so much about us and I know next to nothing about you.'

'Maybe that's the way I like it.'

This was like hammering bricks with a feather. Useless. Still, Jenna wasn't a girl who gave up. Not when she really wanted to know. She'd gained a reputation in nursing circles for helping even the most recalcitrant patients confide their troubles—and trouble was behind this man, Jenna knew for sure. Trouble with a capital T.

Maybe laughter would work. 'Is it dark, brooding and mysterious you're being, Mr Jackson?' she teased. She faced him full on, and with an effort she even made her eyes twinkle. 'Do you yearn to play Heathcliff?'

'To your Cathy?' There was no answering smile. Riley was still and watchful—as though he couldn't make Jenna out, and he didn't trust her one inch. What on earth was the man expecting her to do? she thought ruefully. Bite him?

Jump him?

Ha.

'You have to be kidding,' Jenna managed. 'Heathcliff's Cathy? I have better things to do with my life than pine for lost love and die in childbirth.'

'I'm glad to hear it.' All of a sudden Riley's voice was strained to the point of breaking. 'But I'd prefer a bit less of the curiosity, if you don't mind.'

'You think I'm nosy?'

'You and Maggie.'

'I like Maggie,' she told him. 'I don't even know who she is and I'll bet you're not going to tell me.'

'There's no need to tell you. Why are women so damned curious?'

'We're taught it in girl school,' she flashed. 'Where we're taught that girls like ironing and men like taking out the garbage, but men are otherwise useless. However, at great personal sacrifice, I'll concede that in certain situations men do have their uses. Therefore if I wash, you can wipe. Only I'd prefer you to keep your distance as you do, Mr Jackson. Let's keep our compartments separate.'

'Suits me.'

His voice was light but Jenna flashed him a doubtful glance—and realised he was serious.

Jenna's accusation of categorisation had been made flippantly, but she was astute enough to realise that, for Riley, those categories held truth.

Something in Riley's face said he was stretched tight with the strain of having her close. More. She looked at his face and knew that he didn't want her here. Badly.

She swallowed.

'Riley, would you prefer if Karli and I stayed out of your way today?'

She was right. She knew by the way his eyes flashed to hers that she was right.

But it was stupid and he knew it. He gave her a rueful smile. 'Who's going to tell Karli that she can't hammer?'

'It's me you don't want close, then?'

'I didn't say that.'

'You didn't have to.'

Their eyes locked. He knew what she was saying. They both knew what was the underlying problem here. But there was no future in their attraction, and Karli was here and the whole thing was impossible.

'Okay.' He appeared to regroup and Jenna eyed him with suspicion. Suddenly there was laughter lurking behind his dark eyes. The man was like a chameleon, changing moods on the instant.

'If I keep you here, how about you do the bedrooms while I do the outside work?'

'I beg your pardon?'

'If I seal them on the outside, will you clean them on the inside?'

If he could pretend this thing between them wasn't happening, so could she. 'More dust! And I'm almost clean!'

'Didn't you pack overalls?' he demanded, and sighed as Jenna shook her head. 'Honestly. What tourists pack for this place is hopeless.'

'This place didn't come with a tourist brochure,' Jenna said with dignity. 'I was hoping for something more like a five-star hotel with swimming pool.'

'There's a dam three miles north of here where you can swim.'

'Yeah, right. With sun lounges and fluffy towels and someone serving pina coladas?'

'I could supply a beer.'

Jenna suddenly focussed. He was serious. 'You mean you really can swim there?'

A swim. Water all over her without having to pump like crazy. It sounded…irresistible. 'Are you serious? If we work all day, is there somewhere we can swim tonight?'

'If you don't mind sharing a waterhole with a few cattle,' Riley told her, startled. 'And the odd kangaroo and any other form of wildlife who depend on it. It's not what you might call appealing.'

'If I can swim, then it's definitely appealing.' She eyed him thoughtfully. 'Let's make a deal. Karli and I will work for you all day—I'll even get my shorts dirty in the cause—as long as you take us for a swim tonight.'

'I...'

'It's a great deal,' she said hurriedly, aware that Riley's instinct was to refuse. And she knew why he should refuse. For exactly the same reason she shouldn't ask in the first place.

But there was something within—something growing by the moment—a nagging urgency, saying: Manipulate every second you can to be with this man. This man is important to you. You hardly know why, but your body is giving you all sorts of messages you'd be a fool to ignore.

To go calmly back to England without finding out what those messages could mean—without finding out what could happen—was unthinkable.

So she stood and watched his face and waited and didn't let him off the hook.

'It's not exactly your tiled backyard swimming pool,' he said uneasily. 'We're talking mud.'

'With swimmable water in the middle of mud?'

'Yeah, but...'

'I like mud.'

'You won't.'

'Do you want me to work or not?' Jenna glared. 'I really want a swim, Mr Jackson, and I'm willing to work to get one. I'll forgo luxury towels and the pina colada. But the rest... All you have to do is say yes.'

Their eyes locked—and the message between them was a challenge on Jenna's part, and something she couldn't fathom on Riley's. And finally, inevitably, Riley relented.

'All right, Miss Svenson,' he said slowly. 'You win.' He hesitated, as though already regretting his agreement. 'Mind, I expect hard labour for the luxury of sun, mud and surf.'

'Surf?'

'The water snakes make the surf,' Riley said in a voice that was mock serious. 'When they writhe in unison as they attack your toes, you can almost hang ten in the foam they churn. Are you still sure you want a swim?'

She fixed him with a look. 'Are they poisonous?'

He opened his mouth to say yes, but her look was a challenge and he relented. 'No. But they bite.'

'Have you ever been bitten?'

'No, but I might have been.'

'You mean they're more afraid of us than we are of them.'

'They might be.'

She grinned. She was right to trust this man, she thought. He couldn't lie to save himself.

'We'll swim fast,' Jenna retorted. 'Karli can swim like a fish and so can I. If they do bite us, then we'll die happy, and you wouldn't have said a swim was possible if it wasn't.'

Riley stared at her, baffled. The corners of his mouth were twitching as if he was trying not to laugh, but there was still that deep caution embedded in his eyes. He was like a big cat, Jenna thought, wary of everything, but, deep down, downright dangerous.

'All right, then, Miss Svenson,' he said at last. 'If that's the way you want it, then you'll get your mud-bath. If you work for it.'

Jenna had enjoyed her two days' work with Karli. She enjoyed the work even more now. The steady sound of Riley's carpentry and the interested hum of Karli's gossip was great. It made her feel…at peace? It was weird and inexplicable, but it was a feeling Jenna hadn't experienced before and she was savouring it.

The bedrooms were disgusting. Once more Jenna tied up her hair and attacked the dust with a shovel. Riley came in to help her drag the furniture clear so she could clean without hindrance, and then he disappeared fast. You'll do your work by yourself and I'll do mine, his body language said. We're separate.

Separate was fine by Jenna, she decided. But not very separate. Karli was staunchly with Riley, her allegiance to this wonderful man unswerving, and it was as if by having Karli by Riley's side a little bit of Jenna was there as well.

In the breaks between Karli's questions, Riley whistled a fractured rendition of 'Misty', and Jenna started humming along in her head. The tune stayed there, a comfort all on its own. All morning, down on her hands and knees, scrubbing, she hummed right along.

Towards midday she heaved a bucket of water outside, tripped on the doorstep and her bucket of water poured down her bare legs onto her toes.

She stared down at her dust-and-water-sloshed toes and made a discovery. She was happier doing this than she'd ever been before. What she was doing here was pure fun.

She giggled.

She looked up from her toe contemplation—and found Riley watching her with bemusement.

'You're nuts,' he told her.

'Yep.' She grinned.

'Is your sister always nuts?' he asked Karli, and Karli considered.

'She's funny.'

'She's got really funny toes,' Riley conceded.

Karli followed Riley's gaze to stare down at Jenna's toes. 'Yuk.'

'Yuk's right,' Jenna told them. 'I'm dirtier than you guys. That means I've been working harder so I get to swim the longest.'

'Will you go back to nursing when you leave here?' Riley asked. The question was unexpected and Jenna's smile faded.

'Of course. What else could I do?'

'I bet your patients think you're terrific.'

'Yeah, they love me to bits,' she said dryly. 'I walk toward them with a syringe or an enema and they fall into my arms. Such devotion.'

He grinned, but that quizzical look was back. As if he didn't have a clue what to make of her.

Good. She liked it that he was off balance. He surely had her off balance and that made them quits. She met his look with a trace of defiance.

'Anyway, that's another world,' she told him. 'Another time. What's more important now is that you're shirking work, Riley Jackson. We have a date with a swim this evening. So let's get on with it.'

'Yes, ma'am.'

*   *   *

She had courage.

All day as he worked Riley kept turning Jenna's situation over in his mind. It was none of his business, but he couldn't make his head ignore it. The tilt of her chin, her defiance where other women would have wept, and her capacity for sheer hard work—they combined to make this slip of a girl stand apart.

As she'd stood apart all her life, he conceded, and he found himself growing angry on her behalf.

She didn't seem angry or bitter, though. It seemed Jenna had no wish to punish those who'd made her childhood miserable or who'd put her into this mess.

Riley wanted them punished, though. The more he thought about it, the angrier he grew.

Where the hell was her father? What was this Brian creep doing inheriting money that could make Jenna's life easier?

Riley thumped another weatherboard home with so much force the one above loosened and fell. He wanted to swear, but Karli was sitting in the shade not two yards away, ready to absorb any new and interesting word he might let drop.

A child like this would be such a responsibility, he thought, yet Jenna had taken her on without a thought as to how it could affect her future.

This was nothing to do with him. Butt out of what doesn't concern you, he told himself for the hundredth time. Get this place patched up and get out of here. Get the girl back to England before you go mad. Before you end up where you were before you learned sense.

They worked on, stopping only briefly for lunch. Karli snoozed for a while with her rock, but Riley and Jenna didn't rest. It was as if they were driving each other.

Finally, as the sun lost the worst of its heat even Riley had to admit he was exhausted.

'Okay, Karli,' he told his right-hand man. 'It's swim time.' He walked over to Jenna's side of the house and called. She stuck her head out of the one functional bedroom window and raised an enquiring eyebrow.

'Enough,' he ordered. 'I'm beat.'

'Wimp,' she teased.

Riley stared at her for a long moment. Did she have any idea how beautiful she looked?

Beautiful? How could she be described as beautiful? Covered in dust, her head tied up in rags and framed by a crooked window surround…

Yes, she was beautiful. There was no denying it. Jenna Svenson was lovely.

Hell!

'If you want a swim we have to stop now,' he said and his voice was rougher than he'd intended. 'Anyway, I worked for two hours before you even woke up this morning.'

'More fool you. Come inside and see what I've done.'

He did and was suitably impressed. It was great. It was nearly clean.

'There's a red line around the walls,' Riley told her. 'Is this English fashion? Beige to head height and red above?'

'It's as high as I can scrub,' Jenna said with dignity. 'If you want higher scrubbing, you need to find a higher slave.'

'Hmm.' Riley appeared to check Jenna's diminutive figure—and Jenna flushed under his scrutiny. 'Maybe you're right,' he agreed thoughtfully. 'I do seem to have structural problems with this model.' He managed a twisted grin. 'I wonder how much you'd bring as a trade-in. You're more a sports coupé when I need something like a Ford Bronco.'

Mistake. At Jenna's side was her bucket of water, red with dust. She swooped like lightning, retrieved the rag she'd been using and threw it straight at him. He fielded it like an expert, but water sloshed across his dust-streaked face.

He wiped his eyes with a sleeve—then stood, rag in hand. Considering.

Jenna backed.

'Don't you dare.'

Riley looked again down at his hand, and then across to the dusty figure in front of him. He drew back his hand. Jenna backed some more...

He couldn't do it. He wanted to, but there was a challenge lurking in her lovely eyes that had him retreating.

'Okay, Miss Svenson,' he said softly. Battles were dangerous territory. Battles with Jenna... Yeah, really dangerous. 'I'll let you off the hook just this once.' He paused for a moment, then tossed the cloth back into the bucket. 'There's a spare ladder in the Land Rover.'

'For tomorrow?'

'For tomorrow,' he said firmly. 'We've done more than enough for today. If you have a bathing costume get it on fast. I'll meet you at the Land Rover in two minutes.'

He walked out and left her to it, and only Riley knew just how close a call it had been. Because, instead of hurling sopping rags at the girl before him, it had been the hardest thing he'd ever done in his life to walk away. When all he'd wanted—all his body had screamed at him to do—was to walk over and gather Jenna Svenson to his heart.

The dam was three miles over bumpy track north of the house. The only sign of it as they approached was a decrepit windmill, moving lazily in the hot north wind. It was so late the sun had lost most of its heat, but even so it was hot enough to make a swim seem the most desirable thing in the world. Jenna sat beside Riley in his open Land Rover and her tongue was practically hanging out at the thought.

Same with Karli.

'We're going swimming. We're going swimming,' Karli chortled and her enthusiasm was appreciated by all of them. It eased the awkward silence—the tension that seemed to be building by the moment.

'How come you have a truck here?' Jenna asked, more to break the silence than anything.

'It came with the farm. I spent the first day here getting it back into working order,' he told her.

'So you have a better truck at Munyering?'

'Of course.'

Munyering. What was it like?

What was this man like?

Then they arrived and the questions stopped dead as Jenna gazed out in bewilderment.

This was certainly no luxury swimming pool. Here at last were the cattle Riley had talked about. The beasts stood in a forlorn-looking ring on the edge of the muddy water. There were a hundred or so head of cattle by the look of it—and that was just about all they were. Heads. Skin and bone and not much else. Jenna had never seen such pathetic-looking animals in her life.

'Riley, they're...' Jenna fell silent, aghast. She looked out at the sad-looking animals and her heart lurched within her. Surely these beasts couldn't live here?

Karli had stilled beside her and she knew the child shared her horror.

'I know.' Riley glanced over at Jenna and his look told her he understood what she was feeling. 'They look terrible, and these are dreadful conditions for cattle. But they won't be here much longer.'

'What do you mean? You don't mean...they're dying?'

'They were.' Riley pulled up beside the dam. The cows nearest the truck made a desultory move away—but not too far. It was as if the herd as a whole had simply run out of energy. 'Believe it or not, Jenna, these cattle are on the road to recovery.'

'I don't believe it.'

'Believe it,' Riley said and his voice was suddenly grim. His face tightened. 'I don't want you thinking I caused this. I've only just bought this place. The man who owned it deserves to be shot. He walked off the place, abandoning it with a couple of thousand head of cattle still dependent on him for maintaining their water supply. He went bankrupt—he couldn't afford the fees to transport his cattle to market, so he just left them to rot. When I heard the place was on the market I flew over and found dead and dying cattle everywhere.'

'But how long—?'

'That was three weeks ago.' Riley's voice was still grim.

'I bought the place on the spot—in fact settlement's not until next week, but I've spent the last weeks here getting the water going again. Mending pumps so the bores are flowing. This dam's fed by an underground spring and mostly it's higher than this, but the drought's meant the spring's dried and the water has to be pumped. This dam's fine again, but others further out still need attention. That's why I couldn't leave until now. I've been getting the bores going again and making sure the dams and troughs are full. Some of the cattle were in such bad condition when I found them I had to put them down.'

'But they don't have anything to eat,' Jenna whispered.

'There's forage enough. These cattle are tough. They'll survive here as long as they have water.' Then he managed a smile. 'It's not quite as intensive farming as back home in your Oxfordshire fields, though. If we run one head of cattle per square mile we reckon we're doing well.'

Jenna took a deep breath. One cow per square mile? 'So...so how big is this farm, then?'

'About three thousand square miles.'

'And yours? What did you call it? Munyering?'

'Ten.'

'Ten? Ten what?'

'Ten thousand square miles.'

'Ten thousand square miles!' Jenna did some fast retrieval of schoolgirl maths. 'That's about three hundred miles across by three hundred miles wide.'

'Something like that. It's a bit splodgy at the edges.'

She subsided into staggered silence, the enormity of Riley's landholding leaving her speechless. Yet...if it was all like this, was it worth anything?

The man who'd owned this farm had walked off, and who could blame him?

'I told you,' Riley said gently, watching her face and seemingly guessing her thoughts. 'My farm is better.'

It'd want to be, Jenna thought grimly, but she didn't say it. Instead she looked out again at the cattle. Karli was gazing at a cow with interest and the cow was gazing back, her big brown eyes seeming almost mournful. 'You said these cattle won't be here much longer,' she whispered. She glanced at Karli's cow and then glanced away. 'What did you mean?'

'We'll truck them out,' Riley told her. 'They can survive here but they won't thrive. As soon as the house is habitable I'll send men in to base themselves here while they work. They'll bring trucks, they'll build holding yards and they'll muster this lot. Then they'll bring them back to Munyering where they can recover. There's feed enough on Munyering to make these beasts think all their Christmases have come at once. Munyering is south of here and we're not drought-affected. I said it's better, Jenna. Believe me.'

'But this place is awful. How could it ever have been a farm?'

'It's in drought, Jenna,' Riley told her. He'd drawn to a halt before the muddy bank, a sheet of hoof-marked mud leading to deep water. 'This place isn't always so awful. When the rains come I'll bring cattle back here again. I won't depend on this place for permanent pasture, though. The last owner did that. It worked for five years, but then he lost the gamble. If you gamble with nature you'll always lose. If I can just use it in the good times, though, it makes a decent little addition to my own property.'

A decent little addition. Three thousand square miles. Jenna was trying hard to do some adjusting in her head, but all she could do was boggle.

Karli was trying to outstare the cow. Jenna was doing arithmetic. Riley climbed out of the truck and he grinned at them both.

'Are you guys intending to sit in the truck all evening and commune with nature, or are you serious about that swim?'

Jenna stared out at the cows. The cows stared straight back.

'I'm not sure I can swim with an audience,' she said nervously and Riley chuckled.

'Don't mind them. They'll love it. I bet they've never seen anything like you guys in their lives.'

'This one likes me,' Karli announced.

Jenna still had some qualms.

'Won't we stir up the water? Make it too muddy for drinking?'

'You have to be kidding!' Riley shook his head. 'Lady, until two weeks ago this place was a muddy puddle. The pump had packed up completely and if I'd arrived three days later all these cattle would be dead. What they're drinking now is cattle nectar. Mud and all.'

'I'm not sure I want to swim in cattle nectar.'

'Hey, I've driven three miles in the heat to give you a swim,' Riley retorted, exasperated. 'Now, are you going to get out of this truck and go for a swim or are you not? If not, then stay here while Karli and I swim. Karli, do you want to swim?'

'Will I have to walk through the mud to reach the water?' Karli asked.

'Yes. It'll ooze through your toes.'

'Ooh,' Karli gasped, and bounced out of the truck, heading for oozing mud.

'What about it, Miss Svenson?'

'I'm…I'm swimming.'

'Then do it,' Riley told her. 'Before our audience starts slow-clapping in impatience.'

Going for a swim here wasn't quite as easy as it sounded. Nor was the mud as inviting to Jenna as it was to Karli.

Jenna had her costume on—until now demurely hidden under shorts and shirt. She slipped off her outer garments, took two steps from the truck—and stepped right into a cow pat mixed with mud.

Jenna yelped.

'Lesson one,' Riley said, strolling round the truck to investigate and grinning in appreciation of her problem. 'You're in cattle country now, ma'am. Expect a little dung.'

Jenna stared down at her toes.

'I think,' she said carefully, 'that I'd like to go home now, Mr Jackson.'

'What, back to the house?'

'I mean back to England.'

'Oh, dear.' Riley's laughter was not so subtly hidden behind the concern. 'But now you need a swim more than ever.' He hauled off his shirt and tossed it into the back of the truck. Then his boots. And then his jeans.

It was as much as Jenna could do not to yelp again.

Riley paused. 'Is there something else wrong?' he asked blandly.

'Y...yes.' Jenna swallowed. 'I would have thought...well, you're not exactly decent!'

'I'm wearing shorts.'

'Yeah, but...'

'But what? These are as respectable as swim gear.'

They were too. They were aged boxers. They shouldn't be enough to make her gasp.

Every time she saw this man's body she wanted to gasp.

'When I packed to come here, I thought any possible audience would be cows,' Riley told her. 'If I'd known you were coming maybe I'd have packed my neck-to-knees. But I didn't know, so I didn't bring them.' His eyes ran over her body in its not-so-demure one-piece and his smile deepened. 'And I'm almost as decent as you are. Not as noticeably eye-candy, but almost as decent.'

Then as her colour started to mount he grinned down to Karli who, in her own cute pink bathing costume, was tentatively exploring the mud with one small toe. 'Karli's not shocked. My cows aren't shocked.' He turned again, his gaze cruising from Jenna's toes to her face, his eyes so warm that she felt her blush extend from the toes up. 'I'm not even shocked at what you're wearing,' he told her. 'Just deeply appreciative. May I remind you, you have seen me in less. Get over it.'

Oh, great. She really needed reminding of how much of him she had seen. She was the colour of beetroot. He turned away then, thankfully, so she could get her face together again. But…

She risked another peek.

He was magnificent. His body…

Will you stop thinking like this? she told herself desperately. You're in dangerous territory. You have to walk away from this man.

You shouldn't have come swimming. She was talking to herself.

Of course you shouldn't have come swimming. You shouldn't have even come to Australia. What on earth are you doing, swimming with an almost-naked man in the middle of the Australian Outback—watched by a hundred or more cows?

She had no answer.

There was no answer.

'Come on, Karli. Let's leave your sister to tut-tut over my lack of dress in private.' Riley and Karli were already at the water's edge. Riley was holding Karli's hand, with Karli gasping in delight as mud oozed to their ankles. The mud was surrendering each foot with a delicious slurp as the pair moved forward.

But beyond the mud there was deep water.

She was in deep water already, Jenna thought desperately. Deeper water than she'd ever been in in her life. So…

So Jenna Svenson took a deep breath. She threw caution to the wind and squelched across to the water's edge.

The mud was disgusting, but suddenly she didn't care at all. The water was cool and delicious. She waded in to waist-deep. It was just plain wonderful.

Who needed swimming pools?

Forget how she was feeling, she told herself. Forget Riley.

Her body knifed forward into deep water as caution was thrown away on the hot north wind.

She'd enjoy her swim. She'd block him out somehow.

And if she couldn't?

Whatever.

CHAPTER EIGHT

THE water was unbelievably cool.

Away from the edge, the dam sank to eight or nine feet—deep enough to allow Jenna's whole body to sink. She promptly sank. She stayed under until she ran out of air, then she surfaced and promptly sank again. Karli was safely with Riley so she could concentrate on getting herself cool. On getting herself together.

'Does she always bob up and down like this? It's very distracting.'

He was too close. Jenna surfaced, spluttered and looked wildly round to find Riley's face immediately behind her left shoulder. He was floating on his back, and Karli was seated happily astride his broad chest.

For the life of her she couldn't think what to do. Or what to say.

So she sank again. She stayed under for as long as she could.

When she rose to the surface he was waiting. Riley had swung Karli onto a floating log, and as

Jenna rose he caught her shoulders and held her above the surface.

'This is very unrestful,' he complained.

'Unrestful for who?' she asked breathlessly. 'Let me go.'

'Only if you promise not to sink again. It's making Karli and me nervous. We keep thinking you're being eaten by yabbies.'

'Yabbies?' Unconsciously Jenna's toes lifted so she was floating with drawn-up knees.

'Yabbies.' Riley smiled. 'Little lobsters.' His face was glistening with water, and his streaming hair was plastered in curling tendrils across his forehead. He looked wickedly attractive. And his eyes were inches from hers. Too close for comfort.

Far too close.

And then suddenly he was not close enough for Jenna's liking. There was an almost unbearable temptation to put out a hand and touch that laughing face. To push back the streaming hair. To press herself closer in the water—press herself against her man.

That was how she was thinking of Riley Jackson, she knew, with a sudden fierce realisation of how her heart was working. There was something deep inside that was telling her that Riley was her man. Her home. Whether he knew it or not.

'I'm not scared of yabbies,' she told him. She pulled away, and something of the way she was feeling must have come through. Riley released her and stayed treading water, his face watchful.

'You don't need to be scared of yabbies,' he agreed. 'And you don't need to be scared of me. I won't hurt you, Jenna,' he said softly across the water now dividing them. 'I have no dishonourable intentions.'

I wish you did, Jenna thought desperately. Because I certainly do.

She didn't say it out loud. Instead she managed to smile at Karli, then gave her log a shove that had the little girl sailing across to the far side of the dam. Jenna followed, kicking hard, sending up a spray, propelling the log until she was about twenty feet from Riley. She was trying desperately to make herself relax.

'Push me into the mud,' Karli commanded. 'I need to make mud pies.'

'Certainly, my lady.' She shoved until Karli's craft beached itself. Karli proceeded to roll herself into waist-deep water, scoop up handfuls of mud and arrange them with care on her log-raft.

Karli had always been a self-contained child, a talent born of necessity. She'd never needed to be entertained. It worried Jenna at times, but she'd learned not to press. She didn't press now, even though making mud pies with Karli might have lessened the tension. Instead she lay back in the water, floating with the warmth of the evening sun on her face.

It was glorious.

But all she could think of was Riley.

What if she'd stayed in his grasp? she thought. What if, instead of pulling away, she'd let herself be drawn closer?

Nothing would have happened, she told herself bitterly. How could he be attracted to her? He'd never asked her to come here. And she wasn't exactly free. She had Karli.

She came with strings.

As far as Riley was concerned, Jenna must be a nuisance of an English girl who'd climbed off the train and demanded his help. A nuisance with a child attached who he felt sorry for. And that was it.

Like her, Riley was floating on his back, but he'd remained on the far side of the dam. There as much distance as possible between the two of them. It was the way he obviously wanted it.

But she didn't want distance. She desperately didn't want distance.

What to do about it?

Nothing.

Nothing was for cowards. Nothing was… unthinkable.

Tomorrow morning he'd leave again and be gone for another interminable day. Then he'd put her in his aeroplane and take her back to civilisation. That would be that.

She'd leave here for ever, she thought bleakly. She and Karli would go back to England to her hospital bedsitter, and figure out how she could afford to keep Karli. Her life had been bleak before as she'd struggled to pay off the debts she'd incurred to get her professional qualifications. How much more bleak would it be now?

At least she'd have Karli.

That was a good thought. It settled her. She glanced over at her little sister who was concentrating on mud-pie making as if she were performing brain surgery. Life would be better with Karli.

It'd be even better if she'd never met Riley, she thought dully. If she'd never known such a man existed.

Jenna's eyes left Karli. She very carefully didn't look at Riley, but she let her gaze wander everywhere else.

There were those who would say this was the bleakest place on God's earth. The water she was

swimming in was mud-brown. The dam was surrounded by a low bank of churned-up mud and
there was one ancient, gnarled and very dead tree
nearby. Apart from the dead tree, all that was in
sight was a line of underfed cattle, staring out over
the swimmers with bovine nonchalance.

Plus two small kangaroos, approaching the water
with caution for an evening drink.

This place was the ends of the earth, she thought.
She should welcome the thought of getting out of
here. Of leaving.

Instead Jenna turned back toward Riley and
knew that in leaving it'd be as if she were tearing
her heart from her body.

So do something, Jenna, her inner self told her.

Show him how you feel.

Jenna froze, horrified. She couldn't.

Could she?

But suddenly she couldn't bear not to. After all,
what did she have to lose?

Riley?

She was losing him anyway. He wasn't hers—
except in her heart.

And if, somehow, she could find the courage to
show him…

So Jenna Svenson, quiet, diminutive Jenna,
who'd held herself to herself for the whole of her

life, whose only gambles had led to disaster, took a deep breath, counted to three—and duck-dived under the water straight towards him.

She got it right. Years of visits to unwelcoming parents in five-star resorts, stuck with bored child-minders who'd had the choice of caring for their charge in a hotel room or at the hotel pool—those years had taught both her and Karli to swim like fish. She aimed herself beautifully. There was no way Riley could see her coming.

So Riley knew nothing until Jenna surfaced right underneath him. He jerked sideways in shock. Her breasts slid up against his naked chest and her hands came out to grasp his body, as if to steady herself.

Accidentally maybe, but how carefully planned!

'Hey.' He jerked away and she was forced to release him. 'A whole dam and you crash into me?' he spluttered.

'Sorry.'

He looked at her oddly and she gazed back with nonchalance.

He turned back to his floating.

'You're being incredibly lazy,' she told him. 'You've hardly swum.'

'I've swum enough.'

'You're hardly even wet,' she teased—and she dived straight under him. She grabbed his feet and he was so stunned that Jenna succeeded in pulling him right under. He surfaced, choking and gasping, to find Jenna laughing from two feet away.

'You don't hold your breath very well,' she told him, considering. 'Are you not a good swimmer?'

'You little…'

She eyed him with hope. This man held himself under such rigid control. What she wanted—desperately—was for that control to snap.

'Maybe it's time for us to head back to the house,' Riley said flatly and he turned away.

Was he made of iron?

One last try.

'When you've had a good soaking,' she told him. She duck-dived again, grabbing his feet and hauling him down once more, but this time instead of releasing him she clung like a limpet—holding him under so that he had to twist and grab her and haul her to the surface with him.

It was never a contest. Riley's strength so far outweighed hers that there was no way Jenna could hold him down—but now as they surfaced he was holding her, and she wasn't pushing away. Not when she was so close to him. Not when her body was against his and she knew that she was absolutely right to fight for this. What this man made her feel…

Even if Riley never touched her again, Jenna would remember how it was to touch him like this, she decided. There was a feeling running through her that seemed like an electric charge. But instead of pain, the current was forming colours, so that all the hues of the rainbow were swirling inside her head as Jenna clung to the man she loved as if she'd never let go.

Over and over a tiny prayer repeated itself. Please let him feel it. Please let me not be imagining this. This man is my other half. Let him recognise it. Let him want me just as much as I want him. Tomorrow can take care of itself, if only I can hold this man right now.

She looked up into his wet and streaming face—her body still huddled where he'd hauled her into his arms in self defence.

Please.

And Riley looked down into Jenna's pleading eyes—and she saw his defences crumble absolutely.

Who could resist this? Who could hold themselves apart from this lovely wisp of a girl—this elf, who one moment was a laughing, teasing wanton—and the next a bereft and frightened girl?

Not a girl. No. The woman in his arms was every bit a woman. He felt her soft, voluptuous curves yielding to the hardness of his body and he felt a piercing of new life surging through his veins. Of hope. Of a sudden trust that life could once again hold warmth and intimacy and love.

Crazy thought. Crazy.

Yet who could doubt it? Certainly not Riley. Not here. Not now. He held her, and Jenna looked up, and he knew by her eyes that she was expecting to be pushed away.

Somewhere in his inner consciousness he knew that this was no wanton action on Jenna's part. He knew that she would do this for no other man.

He was under no illusions. No matter how sweet love could be, it wasn't for him. Not for ever.

But for now...

Treading water in his muddy dam, with his cattle watching in silent approval, with Karli calmly playing on the opposite bank, there was no way Riley could reject what Jenna was offering. He stared down into her lovely face and there were no defences. No defences at all.

Jenna. His love?

His love for now.

But maybe now was all that mattered. With infinite gentleness he gathered her closer, willing her body to nestle into his, and he felt her joyful submission with a shard of pure, piercing joy.

It was crazy to feel like this. Yet a man would have to be superhuman to resist—to not want her—to push away what she was offering.

He wanted her so much. He wanted her as a starving man wanted food. More. It was as if his soul had been starved for all these years, and somehow Jenna were feeding it, releasing his soul from its lonely, shrivelling self and letting it burst forth in an explosion of pure joy.

Her hands were on his shoulders, sliding round to hold his muscled body against her, and her breasts were moulding into his chest. He was totally supporting her now. If they sank, they sank together, and at one level a thought shot through him that that was just what they should do. Die now. Die happy.

Which was crazy. A hundred cattle were watching—dependent on him. His responsibility. Karli was making mud pies. Jenna's responsibility. There could only be this one moment, snatched from reality.

But a moment was okay by him. If a moment was all they had, then so be it. He looked into

Jenna's face and found her eyes were glistening with something that wasn't the muddy dam water. Tears? There was laughter, a boldness, echoes of the toughness that had kept her from going under for all those years as she'd fended for herself, but underneath she was soft and aching and as needful as he was.

He wasn't needful.

Liar. Who wouldn't be needful when this woman was in reach? When she was so close and so lovely.

He managed a fleeting glance across at Karli, almost hoping that she needed them. That she could stop what was starting to seem inevitable. But Karli had discovered the kangaroos. She was carrying one of her mud pies out of the water, as if to take it to the animals on the bank.

She was safe and she was occupied.

Back in the water, Jenna watched him. Waiting.

There was no help for it. A man had to do what a man had to do.

'You realise we're playing with fire,' he told her.

'We're in water. We can put any fire out.'

'Are you sure?'

'No,' she admitted. 'I'm not sure of anything. All I know is that I want you.'

'You…'

'Shut up, Riley,' she said softly. 'Just shut up and kiss me.'

So he did. Finally, tenderly, inevitably, Riley did what he had to do. He bent his face and kissed her.

He'd never known such sweetness. Never. Jenna's lips welcomed him with joy. Her tongue came out and tasted, piercing him with a desire that filled his entire body. Her hands held, clung— wanted and wanted…

He'd tugged her out of deep water now, so they were able to stand. Their feet were sinking into mud but it left them free to concentrate on each other rather than staying afloat.

Still they kissed. There were no barriers between them now. The barricades they'd built around themselves seemed to have dissipated in the hot night air, disappearing as if they'd never been. It was as if there'd been some silent exchange of vows.

For this moment, we're one. Pain and separation and the extensions of bleak lives are for tomorrow. For now there's only joy, and that joy has to be taken and grasped with both hands.

Would that this moment could last for ever, Riley thought, dazed beyond belief. This perfection.

He pulled back and found Jenna watching him, her eyes still wet with tears. Was this woman weeping for him?

'Jenna, I don't want to hurt you.'

'Oh, Riley.' Jenna ran her hands through his hair and she leaned forward and kissed him again, lightly and with infinite tenderness. 'Riley, how could you ever hurt me? I love you.'

There. It was out. He gazed at her and saw that she was expecting him to recoil. As he should recoil. But how could he?

'I could love you, too,' he murmured.

I could love you.

It was a possibility. That was all.

Yet still, for now it was enough. Jenna's hands ran through his hair again and again, and she knew there was some deep hurt here. Some hurt that would have to be healed before he could trust.

And if that didn't happen? If she didn't have time? If she and Karli had to board a plane to England in a couple of days and never see this man again?

What then?

Then this would have been worth it, she told herself. She loved him and she'd fight with everything she had. She'd fought for what she needed all her life. This might be the biggest fight of all.

'You are so beautiful,' he whispered. 'To make love to you…'

'Is impossible,' she whispered back and she made no effort to hide her regret. 'Not with my little sister in full view. We've probably shocked her socks off as it is.'

'I don't see any socks—and kangaroos are much more interesting than we are.' Riley glanced across at Karli and his mouth twisted into a smile. 'Though that's not saying we don't have a very interested audience.'

Jenna blinked and checked for herself. He was right. The cows were lined up on the bank, peering down at them with astonishment. Behind them, the kangaroos had grown in number to about thirty. They'd come to the waterhole for their evening drink, but every kangaroo in the mob was staring straight at Jenna and Riley.

'We've shocked the socks off the animal kingdom,' Riley told her, chuckling into her hair. He lowered his mouth so he was kissing the nape of her neck. Sensations of pure light were filtering up from Jenna's toes and flicking back down again, through and through.

She belonged right here, Jenna thought dreamily. In this man's arms. Wherever Riley was, that was where Jenna belonged.

'Why are you kissing Jenna?' It seemed Karli had finally noticed.

Riley pulled away, and with infinite regret Jenna let herself be put at arm's length

'Jenna's worth kissing,' Riley told Karli. 'Don't you think so?'

'Yeah, but that was a really long, slurpy kiss,' Karli told them. 'Do you see the kangaroos, Jenna?'

'Y...yes,' said Jenna.

'Do you want to help me make mud pies?'

'Maybe we should,' Riley said, and Jenna could have screamed.

'In a bit, Karli,' she told her. 'When we finish kissing.'

'The kids at school say you get boy germs if you kiss,' Karli told them. 'And babies.'

'How horrible.' Jenna laughed, but it was a pretty shaky laugh.

'And we wouldn't want boy germs or babies, now, would we?' Riley said and she winced. There was suddenly distance in his voice. As if he'd re-membered something important.

'Um...no.'

'Maybe we'd better go,' Riley said.

'You mean stop kissing?' Jenna asked.

'I think…maybe we're not being wise.'

'Are you afraid of how I make you feel?' she asked—and the whole world held its breath while she waited for the answer.

'I don't do emotion,' he said at last.

'Why not?' This was a crazy time and a crazy place for such a conversation, she thought. They were neck-deep in muddy water. Karli had returned to her pie-making, and all around them were cows and kangaroos having their evening drink.

Surely this conversation shouldn't be so intense?

But it was and they had to see it out.

Riley's defences were back in place, Jenna thought bleakly. What was going on? What was in this man's past to make him react like this?

'You say you love me,' he said, and his voice was suddenly mocking.

'I think…I think that I do.'

'Then you need to do some fast learning.'

'To learn what?' Her eyes weren't leaving his face, and what she saw there made her cringe. She'd fought but she'd lost. His defences were up again and his eyes were bleak and hard.

'Love's only another name for present need,' he told her. 'It assuages loneliness, and that's all it does. It doesn't lock one person to another for ever. Nothing does that.'

How could he say that? That nothing tied one person to another? When she was so tightly bound she felt she'd be ripped apart if she were to leave him.

'How did you learn that?' she whispered.

He shrugged, moving back a step in the water. Extending the distance between them. 'I was a fool. I got married.'

'Oh.'

He looked down at her then, and his face suddenly relaxed into humour. 'There's no need to look like that,' he told her. 'I told you. It's long over. You're not having an illicit embrace with a man with a wife, six kids and a mother-in-law. Lisa left me years ago.'

Jenna swallowed. 'Wh…why?' It was none of her business, but she knew the answer was desperately important.

'People do. They walk away and others hurt. Like us. If we took this anywhere and then broke up, it'd tear Karli apart.'

She stared up in confusion. He'd moved beyond her. 'How could that happen?'

'Everyone leaves this place. No woman can handle the life out here.'

Jenna looked about her—cautiously. 'If you brought your wife here, then maybe you couldn't blame her for wanting a few creature comforts after a while,' she ventured. 'If you brought her to a place like this...'

'Munyering's not like this,' Riley said harshly. 'And she knew...' He stopped, as if thinking better of what he'd started to say. 'This is nothing to do with us. With you. It's been years.'

'But not long enough for you to trust a woman again?'

'Until you came I swore I'd never touch another woman.'

'And now you've touched me. Excellent.' She reached forward, took his face between her hands and kissed him again, hard and deep, searching for the break in his defences. 'So now your vow's broken—what are you going to do with me?' she whispered. 'Send me to the dungeon for tempting a man?'

'It'd be a waste to put you in any dungeon.' His hands gripped her waist, but, instead of gathering her to him again as she so desperately wanted, he set her back from him again. 'No. Jenna, you're enough to make any man break any vow. If Karli wasn't here, and if you hadn't said you loved me, then maybe I'd take you to my bed and we'd have great sex and we'd remember this interlude with pleasure for the rest of our lives.' His gaze was suddenly uncertain. Wistful? As if he was speaking of something that could never be.

'But you have said you love me,' he told her. 'I don't believe it, but I can't think... I can't hurt you. Whatever it means, it can't be allowed to progress any further than it already has. It's not your life you're playing with here, but Karli's.'

Huh? 'Are you saying I'm risking Karli?' Jenna's aching desire was suddenly overtaken by confusion. 'What do you mean?'

'Your responsibility is to Karli.'

Confusion became anger—just like that. 'And I'm risking that by falling in love with you?'

'You don't really love me. You just want—'

'You know nothing about what I want,' she snapped. 'You know nothing about me at all if you think I'd risk Karli in any way. I have no idea why I'm feeling like I'm feeling about you. I only know that I am. So now I've told you. I'm honest. Not like you, Riley Jackson, who can't even admit to himself what he's feeling.'

'I don't—'

'You do,' she snapped. 'I can feel what you feel. I'm not some teenage twit with a crush. I have no idea what's between us, but I do know that I've never experienced it before and it's special and it's brilliant and you're not brave enough to even take the first step to trying to figure out where this could take us.'

'I don't want—'

'To take risks,' she flashed.

'And you do?' Anger was meeting anger. 'Of course you do. You're a born risk-taker. Getting off a train in the middle of nowhere even if it means risking your sister's life.'

What was he saying? She couldn't believe it. Her hand came back to slap the accusation from his harsh, unyielding face.

She caught herself. No.

She wanted to slap him. More than anything else she wanted to pierce that accusing harshness. And if she did…

Maybe it could work. Maybe. But Karli was on the other side of the dam. To resort to physical aggression was never appropriate, but how much more inappropriate now.

'Fine,' she said grimly and turned away to trudge out of the dam. 'If that's the way you want to think of me, then it's okay by me. Karli and I are getting out of here as soon as possible, and you'll never see us again.'

'Do you want to catch the train tomorrow instead of flying out with me?'

That made her pause. The train.

Yes. She did want to catch the train. She desperately wanted to walk away. Her humiliation was threatening to overwhelm her and she could cope with a few reporters if the alternative was more humiliation.

But then her eyes flew to Karli.

Karli was starting to be happy again. The little girl had faced so much. How much more could she stand?

'No,' she whispered. 'I…please.' She'd risked too much. She'd risked Karli's well-being just by being attracted to him. She'd forgotten how dependent they were on this man.

There was a moment's loaded silence. She met his look and held it and something of what she was feeling must have come through. She saw his expression turn to rueful, as if he too was remembering what else she was facing.

'I won't put you on the train.' His gaze shifted to Karli and there was suddenly a real remorse in his tone. 'Hell. I'm sorry that I implied you'd put Karli at risk. It was a stupid thing to say and I had no right to say it.' He hesitated. 'But I need to put you away from me, Jenna. I don't do relationships.

I'm on my own. You're with Karli and I'm here. There's no meeting place. Not in a million years.'

Not in a million years.

Jenna nodded. Bleakly. Maybe Riley was right. He didn't want her in his world and she had no right to ask to be included.

But it was so hard.

What she was feeling was love. She knew it. She'd never felt like this before, but now the sensation threatened to overwhelm her. Her love might be transient, she thought bleakly. It might be based on present need, but her heart swelled with pain at what he was saying.

There's no meeting place.

She could do no more. She'd thrown her pride to the wind. She'd thrown herself at him and exposed herself to pain and to rejection as she'd done to no one in her life. There was nothing more she could do.

'Thank you for our swim,' she said dully. 'We loved it. Maybe you're right, though. Maybe it's time to go back to the house.'

'I'm sorry, Jenna.'

She looked at him then—really looked at him— and her chin tilted upward. *He* was sorry. 'Coward,' she whispered.

'I'm not a coward. I don't want to hurt you.'

'You don't want to be hurt yourself.'

'Maybe.' His face closed. 'Whatever. You're right. It's time we went home.'

He turned and strode out of the water, up the bank and across to where Karli was offering mud-pie sandwiches to cows.

'Are you ready to go home?' he asked her and she raised her face to his and smiled.

'Okay. Have you finished kissing Jenna?'

'Yes, I've finished kissing Jenna.'

'Good, 'cos it looked pretty yucky to me.'

'Yep.' He glanced across at Jenna and his face closed even further. 'We never should have done it.'

CHAPTER NINE

THEY hardly saw him then until late the next afternoon. Riley drove them back to the house, grabbed his swag and a few supplies, and he was gone.

They were left to fend for themselves.

As they'd always fended for themselves.

'Did you guys have a fight?' Karli asked, and Jenna shook her head. She was making them dinner, fighting back tears; trying to make herself angry instead of desolate.

'What makes you think we had a fight?'

'Riley stopped smiling. You stopped smiling.'

'Maybe it's because we're leaving tomorrow. It's making us sad.'

'Do you think we'll ever see Riley again after tomorrow?'

'Probably not.'

'That's really sad.' Karli looked down at her precious rock. 'I'd rather have Riley even more than my rock.'

Jenna tried to pull herself together. She sniffed and tried for a mature, adult approach to what was happening. 'You shouldn't call him Riley. His name's Mr Jackson.'

'He said I could call him Riley. He's my friend. I think we should stay with him for longer.'

'So do I,' Jenna admitted sadly, abandoning mature as being just plain impossible. She and Karli seemed of an age. They surely thought the same. 'But some things just aren't going to happen.'

Karli slept, but there was little sleep for Jenna that night. She lay awake, staring out at the stars in the outback sky, trying to make sense of how she was feeling—of what she'd done. Of how she'd face the future.

There were questions everywhere. There were no answers.

The next day they woke to silence. They threw themselves into more work, fixing the bedrooms up, rigging a device so they could scrub higher than the original dust mark.

It wasn't so much fun without Riley.

In the early afternoon they went outside and saw the far-off sight of the silver train they'd abandoned four days ago. They watched it slow to a stop at the siding to let the other train go through. They watched it leave.

Maybe they should have gone on the train regardless, Jenna thought. Maybe she shouldn't trust Riley to do what he said he'd do.

But she did trust him. He was totally dependable, she knew. Totally dependable, but totally isolated.

He was breaking her heart.

At four she and Karli called it quits. The joyous enthusiasm with which they'd tackled their work over the last three days was completely gone and Jenna was bone-tired. It was as much as she could do to manage the pump.

There was no light-hearted singing of sea shanties.

They washed and they waited.

At five the Land Rover appeared from the south and Riley walked into the house looking worse than Jenna had ever seen him. She might be tired, but he looked exhausted to the point of collapse.

'Riley,' she whispered as he walked in the back door, but his look held her back. It stopped her saying anything else.

'I've finished doing what needs doing,' he told them, his voice drained of emotion. 'Can you be ready to leave in fifteen minutes?'

'We're packed already,' Karli told him, casting a dubious look from Riley to Jenna and back again.

'That's good,' Riley said and smiled at her.

He didn't smile at Jenna.

The plane bumped down the makeshift runway and rose into the sky, then banked and turned so they were facing south. Riley's face was grim and he stayed silent. Karli was hugging her rock as if she needed its security.

Jenna put her face against the window and stared down at the receding dot that was Barinya Downs.

It was a dump.

She'd fallen in love with it.

She'd fallen in love with Riley.

They should talk, she thought dully. She should be talking to Karli. They should pretend this was exciting. They were flying in a tiny plane over a place as strange as she'd ever been in. They should be acting as if this were an adventure.

It wasn't. Even Karli's face was tight with strain.

Even Karli knew what they were losing, she thought bleakly.

The further they flew south, the greener the country grew and a little over half an hour's flight saw them descend to a place that, after Barinya Downs, looked almost like paradise.

Munyering.

She couldn't believe it. As the plane came in to land she cast a doubtful look across at Riley, but his face was still set and grim. Karli was gazing down with her mouth wide open and Jenna felt like doing the same.

Okay, she did do the same.

It was still dry country—there were no lush, closely fenced fields like home—but this was no dust bowl. The paddocks were dotted with dams, each much larger than the one they'd swum in at Barinya Downs, and most of them ringed by trees. The soil looked rich and red, and there were low blue mountain ranges in the far distance. The paddocks were wide swathes of green pasture. Crops? Even from this height Jenna could see flocks of cockatoos wheeling and squawking about the trees, and there were cattle resting in the shade.

And the house. It was a sprawling white weatherboard farmhouse, surrounded by outbuildings that looked substantial and well cared for. The house was ringed by a wide veranda and a lush garden. Some sort of vine covered the veranda with great looping clouds of purple blossom.

And there was a swimming pool. The pool was a magic blue teardrop nestled into the garden and from the air it looked like someone's version of paradise.

'It's really pretty,' Karli breathed, and Jenna could only agree. She glanced across at Riley and looked away again. His face was a rigid mask. He was fighting with himself, she thought.

'Hey, lighten up,' she told him, fighting her own misery to try and reach him. 'How can you look miserable when you're coming home to this? I know you'll miss your dust, but this is ridiculous.'

He managed a smile, but only just.

'I need to concentrate on landing,' he said, and Jenna bit her lip.

'Of course you do,' she said cordially. 'You need to concentrate on anything that isn't us.'

Riley's silence was made up for by Maggie. As the aeroplane rolled to a halt the lady was waiting and Jenna guessed at once who she was. She looked like a Maggie. A little, dumpy woman in her late fifties or early sixties, she had deep black, wild, frizzy hair, tugged into a knot on top of her head, but with curls escaping every which way. She was wearing a bright red skirt, a bright yellow blouse and a stripey pinafore that was liberally sprinkled with something that looked like flour.

She beamed a welcome as Riley climbed from the plane, but her eyes were already on Jenna and Karli.

'It's true,' she breathed as Riley hauled open the passenger door so they could climb out after him. 'The radio's been full of gossip about these two. You have them safe.' She smiled at both of them and her smile was a caress all on its own. 'Oh, you poor lambs. The fuss... And Riley found you in that heat. Riley, you should have brought them home straight away.'

'I couldn't,' he said shortly. 'The cattle were dying.'

Maggie looked at him then—really looked at him—and Jenna saw her shock as she registered the exhaustion and the strain and the fierce containment. The woman drew in her breath, made to say something—and then seemed to change her mind. She gave him a long, searching look and then turned back to the visitors.

'Come into the house,' she told Jenna. She smiled down at Karli. 'You must be Karli. You know there hasn't been a little girl here for a very long time. You're very welcome.'

'Would you like to see my rock?' Karli asked, and Maggie beamed.

'Of course I would.'

'Is Max free to take these two straight on to Adelaide?' Riley's question was brusque, and Jenna froze. She looked across at Riley.

'I thought...'

'Aren't you taking us?' Karli asked.

'I have work to do,' he told her. 'Max is my overseer—he's Maggie's husband. He has his pilot's licence.' Then, as Karli looked dubious, he smiled at her. 'You'll like Max. He likes kids and I bet he'll like your rock.'

But Maggie was staring at him, seemingly astounded. Seemingly confused.

'Riley, what are you talking about? Max isn't taking anyone to Adelaide tonight.'

'Why not? He can stay overnight and come back tomorrow.'

'He can't.'

'Maggie—'

'There's not enough light,' she said flatly. 'You know he hates flying blind.'

'Oh, come on, Maggie. It's a great night. A full moon and no clouds.'

'He's not doing it.'

'Why the hell not?' He caught himself and cast a glance at Karli, who was gazing straight at him. 'I mean…he'll be fine. He's flown the plane in a lot worse conditions than tonight.'

'Not unless he has to, and tonight he doesn't have to. He's my husband and I say he's not doing it.' Maggie drew herself up to her full five feet two inches and she glared. 'I don't often put my foot down, Riley Jackson, but I'm putting it down now. You let these two mites sleep here for the night. They look almost as tired as you and that's saying something. I'll talk to Max and maybe he can fly them south in the morning.'

'I employ Max,' Riley growled, and Maggie gave him a long, thoughtful look.

'So you do. Just like you employ me. But you won't employ either of us if we quit, which we just might do if you make him do that.'

'Hey,' Jenna said. Things were starting to sound crazy. 'I don't...it doesn't matter.'

Maggie put her hands on her hips and planted her feet apart, pugnaciously standing her ground. 'It does matter,' she retorted. 'Riley's being ridiculous.' She turned to face him again. 'You go in and get yourself clean and dressed and ready for dinner and cut it out with this nonsense. Dinner'll be on the table in half an hour.'

'I'll eat with the men.'

'What the...?'

'Feed Jenna and Karli, Maggie,' he told her, and he turned away as if weariness had suddenly overtaken him completely. 'Give them a bed for the night. Max can take them on in the morning.'

It was the start of a really strained evening.

Maggie took them through to a guest bedroom that normally would have had Jenna exclaiming in delight. Twin beds with mosquito-net canopies, luxurious bedding, a vast overhead fan that wafted the warm air gently around the big room, French windows leading out to the veranda and to the pool beyond. It was truly magnificent, but Jenna hardly saw it.

Maggie seemed distracted. She fussed over them a little, but left as soon as she could so they could shower and change. They used the *en suite* bathroom, which was lovely—but both of them missed their pump. Even clean hair gave minimal pleasure.

Karli was back to being quiet again. She hardly spoke as they dressed and went through to dinner.

The little girl grew even quieter when she realised their dinner was to be taken in solitary splendour—in a dining room that was beautiful but overpoweringly formal and more suited for twelve people than for two.

Maggie flew in and out with their dinner—magnificent steak and fresh salad and a lemon tart that would normally have made both their mouths water. Maggie looked at them with worry in her eyes but she, too, hardly spoke. Her bubbly personality seemed to have disappeared.

We should have caught the train, Jenna thought drearily. This was well nigh unbearable.

After dinner there was no one around at all. The house seemed deserted. They carried their plates through to the big farmhouse kitchen, but even Maggie had now disappeared.

They drifted back to their bedroom, feeling lost. Jenna put Karli to bed.

'Riley doesn't like us any more,' Karli whispered, and Jenna hugged her and told her of course he did, he was just tired.

She didn't believe it. She comforted Karli, but she needed comfort herself.

With Karli finally asleep she went outside to sit on the veranda. Here at least she could look up into the same sky she'd looked at for the last few days. Tomorrow she'd be back in the city and this would be over.

The night was beautiful. Munyering was beautiful, she thought. It was the loveliest place she'd ever been in—a magic mix of outback dreaming and delicious comfort.

Why on earth had Riley's wife ever walked from this?

Where was everyone? The place seemed almost ghostly.

A dog appeared from the shadows, a three-quarter-grown collie. Jenna clicked her fingers and the pup wriggled in delight and slunk forward to have his ears scratched. Any company was welcome. She could go nuts, she thought. Where was Riley?

This was hardly a hospitable end to their stay. Maybe she should be angry. But then, she had foisted herself onto him, she conceded. He'd already done more than he'd had to in helping her. He'd fed her and housed her and he was organising a flight to Adelaide. How could she ask more of him than that?

How could she not?

'Does he talk to you?' she asked the pup.

'No.' The woman's voice came out of the shadows and she turned to find Maggie watching her from behind the gnarled wisteria trunk. 'Riley talk to a dog?' she said bitterly. 'He might get attached and that would never do.'

'I'm sorry.' Jenna started to rise, but Maggie signalled her to stay where she was.

'Don't get up. I need to talk to you.'

'I didn't want to disturb you.'

'You're not disturbing me,' Maggie told her. 'You're disturbing Riley and that's what I want to talk to you about.'

'Well, if you want me to apologise for that...'

Maggie managed a worried smile. 'No. Of course I don't want you to apologise. The opposite, in fact. Riley hasn't been disturbed for a very long time and this is way overdue.'

'What's overdue?'

'Falling in love.'

'Um...' Jenna stared at Maggie, stunned.

Maggie gazed right back.

Jenna broke the look first, turning to gaze out over the swimming pool. There were tiny insects just above water-level and swallows were swooping in and out of the light to snatch their evening meal. A mass of roses grew almost wild on the other side of the pool. A huge overhead sprinkler sent water drifting across the garden in a long, lazy, arcing spray, and the smell of the damp roses was everywhere.

'Who said anything about falling in love?' Jenna whispered.

'Are you in love with him?' Maggie asked.

'I might be.' What was the use of denying it?

'Well, he's sure as eggs in love with you.'

'I don't think so.'

'Have you seen his face?'

'I...'

'Of course. You don't know enough of him to realise.' Maggie took a deep breath and plumped herself down on the bench beside Jenna. 'I'm sorry, Jenna. I don't know whether I'm coming or going.

From the minute he got off that plane and I saw his face... I haven't seen that look since his father died and it made me feel ill.'

'I don't understand.'

'Well, maybe you ought,' Maggie said resolutely. 'You can't fight without weapons, is what I always say. I've been talking to my Max and he says I should butt out of what's not my business, but when have I ever? Did you know Riley's mother walked out on him?'

Jenna was having trouble keeping up. 'No, I—'

'When he was four,' she said, turning to watch the swallows herself. 'Riley's dad was hopelessly in love with her, but she was a spoiled little princess. She came here and he gave her the world, but it wasn't enough. They had three kids—two girls who were older than Riley. Then she met some millionaire at a race meet and she walked away without a backward glance. She broke his father's heart and, as far as I know, Riley never saw her again.'

'Oh, no.'

'Yeah, but that was just the beginning,' Maggie said grimly. 'The girls were just as bad. Riley's sisters. Sure, their mother had walked out on them, but they were older and she'd taught them to be just like her. They didn't like the School of the Air we have here, so they went to boarding-school. They came home when they had to, but they hated the place. By the time Riley was eight they were gone completely. Leaving heartache behind. Riley's father tried hard to keep them together, but it didn't work. So Riley was left with his father, who was just bereft. He died when Riley was eleven.'

Jenna didn't respond. She couldn't. But Maggie looked across at her face in the moonlight and appeared to find what she saw there satisfactory. She gave a decisive little nod and went on regardless.

'It was hell for him,' Maggie said bluntly. 'No one came near him. Not his mother. Not his sisters. Max and I were here, of course, and we made sure they were contacted when his father died, but the only thing they wanted to know was how much they'd inherit. They got enough, but the farm was left to Riley. After all, the farm was all Riley had. Max and I had to apply to be appointed his guardians as there was no one else for him.'

'Oh, Maggie.'

Maggie's hand came across and covered hers, sensing that Jenna was too shocked to say anything else. 'I'll make this fast,' she said. 'Riley kept himself to himself. He's worked and worked. He's learned to play the stock market and he's made this place fantastic. He's one of the wealthiest farmers in Australia now—one of our few millionaires. But six years ago he met Lisa. He met her at a stock sale in Adelaide. She was the daughter of a stock agent, she was gorgeous, she was funny, he married her. But I reckon one of the reasons he chose her was that she was self-contained. Self-containment…it's the one thing he's learned to value above everything. He doesn't trust loving and why should he? Anyway, Lisa didn't help one bit. She left with one of the few men Riley counted as his friend, and she bled him dry in the process. And that's it. Since Lisa left he's refused to even get attached to a dog.'

There was a moment's silence as Maggie reached over to fondle the pup's ears. Then she gave a sniff that was decidedly watery. 'He's worked himself into the ground,' she said. 'He cares for the farm and nothing else. He's committed himself to nobody. And then you came.'

'I…'

'Tonight he's looking like he did the night his father died,' Maggie said. 'You can't leave.'

'Do you think I want to?'

'No,' Maggie said softly. She thought about it for a minute and then corrected herself. 'Oh, I did. I took one look at his face and I thought he'd fallen for someone else who didn't need him. That was why…that was why I left you alone at dinner. I was so upset. But it was also why I refused to let Max take you to Adelaide tonight. I had to figure things out. I had to see.'

'So now you see?'

'Of course I see. I've been talking to him.'

'You're kidding,' Jenna said. 'Riley doesn't let people speak to him.'

Maggie managed a shaky smile. 'No, but if provoked he gives you information. And I've done some provoking. I told him that I was sorry I objected to Max taking you on to Adelaide tonight. I told him I've been listening to gossip over the radio and it seems you're a spoiled little tart who's just as scatty as your mother. Then I stood back and watched.' Her smile grew a trifle rueful. 'He gave me the reaction I wanted. I think if I was a man I would have been slugged.'

'So…' Jenna took a deep breath and tried to focus. 'So what?'

'So he's in love with you. And you're in love with him.' Maggie's smile grew a little more secure. 'I'm not sure what magic happened over the last four days. But was it? Was it magic?'

'It was,' Jenna conceded and Maggie's smile grew broader.

'There. If you think four days at Barinya Downs is magic, then you're perfect for him. Compared to Barinya Downs, this place is a palace.'

'This place is certainly a palace.'

'Then you can stay here for ever.'

'Oh, right. As if he'll let that happen.'

'Go to him,' Maggie urged. 'I've fought hard for an extra night for you. Make it work. He's over in the hangar giving the plane the once-over for the morning. Go and talk to him.'

'I can't.'

'He's not worth fighting for?'

'Maggie, I threw myself at him last night,' she admitted. 'I can hardly humiliate myself any more.'

'I'm not asking you to humiliate yourself. I'm simply asking that you go and talk to him. I don't know...thank him for the stay or something. Provoke him. Push him. Chances are he'll disappear before daylight tomorrow and you won't get a chance to see him then. Just...just try. What have you got to lose?'

Her pride, Jenna thought. But then...did she have one speck of pride left?

'I could do that,' she whispered.

'Well, what are you sitting here for, girl?' Maggie retorted. She grabbed the pup, who was sitting on Jenna's feet. 'Clear the way, pup. The lady has a mission.' She squeezed Jenna's hand. 'Good luck, my dear. Oh, good luck.'

It wasn't going to work.

Jenna walked into the hangar and Riley turned to see who was approaching and his face shut down just like that.

She didn't have a hope.

'I thought you'd be in bed,' he said shortly and she winced.

'I came to thank you for your hospitality.'

'You're welcome.' He turned back to his engine and she stared at him in dismay. And in building anger.

'I'm not,' she said at last, and he turned again.

'Pardon?'

'I'm not the least bit welcome. You can't wait to be shot of me.'

'I didn't say that.'

'You didn't have to.' Then, as his face closed even more she felt herself snap. Damn losing more pride. He needed to be kicked! 'You're being a selfish, unmitigated bore. I have no idea why I even thought I could possibly be in love with you.'

There was a moment's silence. He carefully wiped oil from his hands with a rag, and then put the rag down as if he were afraid it might break.

'An unmitigated bore?'

'Yes.' She stood her ground and flashed fire. 'And you've upset Karli. She doesn't have a clue why you're being so mean.'

'I'm not being mean. I brought you here. I'm arranging for you to be taken to Adelaide.'

'I thought that,' she said. 'I told myself that you're being good to us and I shouldn't complain. But then I figured that you're only giving us things that anyone with money could throw at us. Nicole used to put us up in five-star hotels and provide us with babysitters, too. No one ended up loving Nicole. Not even her daughters.'

'What are you saying?'

'That you're rejecting our love.' How about that for a bald statement? It was true, though, so why not say it?

'I don't want anyone to love me,' he told her, and her anger increased.

'Of course you do. You just won't admit it because you've been hurt in the past. Well, you're looking at an expert at being hurt, and yet here I am throwing my heart stupidly, wantonly at some selfish oaf of a man who won't even take a day off to fly us to Adelaide.'

'Stop it, Jenna.'

'Why should I stop it?' She was past caring, she thought dully. She'd not meant to say any of this, but he stared at her with eyes that were blank, as if he was trying to shut her out, and she couldn't bear it. She could see behind that blankness. He thought that if he let himself love her, then she'd hurt him—just as all those people had done in the past.

'Coward,' she whispered.

'I'm not a coward. I'm a realist.'

'You think what's between us has to end?'

'Of course it has to end.'

'Of course it does,' she said cordially. ''Til death do us part. See, I even know the relevant vow. Death happens to everyone, but I'm banking on fifty years in the interim.'

'You're saying you want to marry me?' he demanded, startled.

They were twenty feet from each other, with the concrete hangar floor stretching out between them. Overhead was a glaring fluorescent light, harsh and almost surreal in the echoing hangar. Hardly the place for a proposal of marriage.

'I'm saying how I feel about you,' she told him. 'That's how I feel. Why not be honest? Marriage or not, you're a part of me. But you haven't the courage to see it.'

'Jenna, it's impossible.'

'Why is it impossible?'

'It won't last.'

'Will you stop it?' She felt like stamping her foot in rage and, dammit, she did. 'You're saying our love can't last so you'll end it now. That's terrific reasoning—I don't think. That's like looking at a table loaded with food and saying you'll be hungry in the future so you won't eat now.'

'I—'

'What's the difference?' she demanded and tilted her chin. 'What's the difference, Riley Jackson?'

'I don't want…'

'To commit. No. I can see that.'

'This is stupid.'

'It is, and it's not my fault that it's stupid.'

'Jenna, go to bed. I'll not risk your happiness. Karli's happiness.'

'Our happiness depends on you, you dopey—'

'Jenna, don't.'

'You're telling me to go away.'

'Yes.'

'Maggie says you love me.'

'Maggie doesn't know.'

'Doesn't she?' She walked a couple of steps forward and faced him square on. 'So she's wrong?' she demanded. 'You can stare straight into my eyes and say she's wrong. That I'm mistaken? That it's totally one-sided and you don't love me.'

He bit his lip and stared at her. 'I don't...'

'You don't what? You don't love me? Say it, Riley.'

'Go to bed.'

'Say it, Riley.'

'Hell, will you get out of my hangar?'

'You can't say it, can you?'

'It doesn't make one whit of difference what I can or can't say. I'm not in the market for another relationship. Please...say goodbye to Karli for me. Tell her I'll write to her when you're back in England.'

'Big of you.'

'It's all I'm prepared to do, Jenna.'

She closed her eyes. Where could she go from here?

Nowhere. Not when he stared at her with eyes that were blank and cold.

Where was his warmth now? Where was the Riley she'd fallen in love with? Where were his chuckle, his smile, his caring?

He'd never given them to her.

So she'd lost, but at least she'd tried. She'd go back to England. She'd fought with everything she had. She could do no more.

'Fine,' she said again. 'Break your heart. Break mine and break Karli's. See if we care.'

And she turned and stalked out of the hangar with her head held high.

From the back she looked almost in control.

But only from the back.

He had to finish checking the engine. But not yet. For now he stood and gazed out into the night and pain echoed round and round in his head.

Coward.

He was, he thought. But…it wasn't just him he was protecting.

He honestly didn't know whether he was capable of giving what they wanted of him.

Husband to Jenna. Father to Karli. From self-containment to family man just like that.

The pup slunk into the hangar and sidled his way up to him and Riley found himself patting him before he knew what he was doing.

The pup. What was his name?

He didn't name dogs. The men had dogs and this was the product of Max's bitch and one of the itinerant drover's dogs. The rest of the litter had been sold, but Max had decided to train this one. The only problem was that the pup had decided that

Riley was the answer to a dog's prayers and when Riley was around he'd go to no one else.

'Leave it, mate,' Riley said bleakly as Jenna disappeared into the darkness. He pushed the collie away. 'I'm not worth loving.'

The pup whined and pushed his nose into the small of his hand.

Riley ignored him.

The pup whined again.

'Enough.' Riley grabbed the keys to the nearest Land Rover. Max could finish the plane. He'd only been using it as an excuse to stay away from the house and he suddenly wasn't far enough away. 'I'm going to check the cattle down south. I'll radio in to let everyone know where I'm gone and I won't be back until after they've left.'

He was talking to a dog?

The dog looked up at him, his head cocked to one side, and Riley could almost swear he understood.

It took him ten minutes to collect what he needed—a swag, and basic food—and write a note for Maggie. He thought of writing a note for Jenna but, hell, what was a man to say?

Nothing. There was nothing left to say.

He climbed into the truck and gunned the motor into gear. But he'd left the passenger window open.

And as the truck started to move, a black and white shape launched itself upward, and the next moment the pup of no name was wriggling his joy on Riley's knee.

He should throw him out.

The pup licked his hand.

'All right,' Riley said, goaded. 'Okay. One dog. But nothing else. Nothing? You hear?'

The pup moved to his knees, slurped him from chin to eyelid, and settled back on the passenger seat with an air of absolute contentment.

Riley could have sworn that the dog grinned.

He didn't do attachment.

He didn't.

CHAPTER TEN

'IT'LL be fine. We'll be fine.'

Jenna held Karli as close as their seat belts allowed. Max was in front of them in the pilot's seat and Riley's home was a fast-receding scene below them. They were headed for Adelaide.

'I won't be fine,' Karli said stubbornly. 'I wanted to stay with Riley.'

'You know we can't do that.' Heck, why was it so hard to make her voice work? All she felt like doing was crumpling into a small soggy ball.

She couldn't. She had to be cheerful and optimistic and she had to plan some sort of future. Somehow.

'We'll catch a plane to Perth so that we can use our tickets back to England,' she told Karli. 'I'll contact Nicole's agent. Maybe she can organise us to stay in Perth for a night or two before we leave.'

'What would we do in Perth?'

'We could take your rock to the museum,' Jenna told her, trying to sound resolute. 'That's what Riley suggested we do—remember? We could get them to tell us exactly what it is.'

'We can't do that.' Karli sniffed and her voice wobbled.

'Why not?'

'I left my rock back at Riley's.'

'Oh, no.'

She hadn't checked. Oh, heck, she hadn't checked. The rock had hardly been out of Karli's hands since Riley had given it to her. Jenna had just assumed she had it with her. She'd been so distressed herself that she hadn't noticed the little girl's hands were empty. Now she stared down at Karli with dismay and thought about the impossibility of asking Max to turn back.

'Oh, heck, Karli,' she said. 'We'll have to phone Maggie and ask her to send it on.'

'No,' Karli said, and Jenna blinked.

'No?'

'I left it behind on purpose,' Karli said, and her voice suddenly stopped wobbling. 'I gave it to Maggie to give to Riley.'

But there the resolution ended. She stared up into Jenna's confused face and her tiny face crumpled into tears.

'I left it behind for Riley,' she wailed.

Riley hadn't needed to camp out. He'd lain awake all night, staring at the stars. The pup had wiggled down into the swag and he'd hugged him, helpless in the face of his need for comfort. 'I can't trust myself,' he told the dog. 'I don't do commitment. Hell, if I were to let myself go there... I'd be a father. If Jenna and I split up—and we would— where would that leave Karli?'

There were no answers. He lay in his swag until he watched the dawn and when finally he saw the little plane lift off from the homestead and head south—not over him as he'd carefully gone north— he made his way home.

Maggie was waiting. The moment he walked in the kitchen she handed him the rock.

Her face was coldly accusing.

'She left it for you,' she told him. 'Poor wee mite.'

He gazed at it blankly.

'Karli's rock.'

'Yep.'

'She left it behind.'

'She gave it to me to give to you.'

'It was my gift to her,' Riley said, still confused, and Maggie sniffed. Every inch of her was vibrating with disapproval.

'Was it now? Well, then, she's given it back.'

'I didn't want it back.'

'There's a lot you don't want, if you ask me.'

'What do you mean by that?'

'You know very well what I mean, Riley Jackson,' she snapped, and turned to take out her fury on some hapless potatoes.

'She loved this rock,' Riley said, staring down at the little starfish and then turning it over to trace the mollusc. They were shiny clean—scrubbed with Jenna's soap.

'That's why she gave it to you,' Maggie said— and sniffed over her potato peelings.

'I don't understand.'

'She said…' Maggie sniffed again and then it was too much. She hauled a handkerchief out and blew her nose with a sound that could be heard in the next state. 'She said that she had Jenna to love her, and you didn't even like your puppy, so you needed her rock more than she did.'

Riley stilled.

Maggie sniffed again.

'You think I've been a fool?' Riley said.

'I don't just think it.' Maggie sliced a potato in two. And then into four. She stared at it a moment longer and then started stabbing the potato any which way. Potato wedges became potato chips and then potato slivers.

'Maggie, I don't know the first thing about being a husband.'

'So don't be a husband. Just love them to bits and let the rest take care of itself.'

'They've gone. It's over.'

'It's only over if you let it be over. Call them back. Max is on the radio.'

'Oh, sure,' he said, goaded. 'Have Max turn the plane and bring them back so we can discuss things? Take things right out of their control? They've had so much happen to them, those two. Jenna was furious at me last night. Do you think I can calmly call Max and tell him to bring her back because maybe I need to talk things through. I don't think so.'

'What are you saying? *Maybe you need to talk things through?*' Maggie eyed him with almost speechless incredulity. 'Talk things through!' She wheeled to face him, still holding her knife. She stared down at the knife, glanced back at her massacred potatoes and then carefully laid her weapon down—as if she just might do something she could regret. After all, these were innocent vegetables who hadn't done anything to anyone.

They weren't Riley.

She regrouped. Sort of. 'All I know is that you're being a dope, Riley Jackson,' she said softly. 'You have to do something.'

And then she stilled.

From the distance came the sound of a plane.

'It can't be,' Riley said. 'I...it'd be stupid. They wouldn't come back.' He shoved the rock into his pocket as if he were thrusting away a dream.

'It's you who's stupid,' she snapped. She listened for a bit more and the momentary relief in her face disappeared. 'No. You're right. That's not our plane. It's someone else.'

Maggie walked to the kitchen door and peered out.

A fiery red little plane—a two-seater with twin engines—was approaching the runway. Gleaming and new, it was totally unfamiliar.

It wasn't alone in the sky. There was another plane coming in to land behind it. A battered, ancient hulk.

'That's Bill and Dot Holmes's plane,' Maggie said.

Bill and Dot were his neighbours at Barinya Downs. Riley frowned, almost distracted. What were Bill and Dot doing here? Bill hated leaving his property.

'Well, don't just stand there,' Maggie said, shoving him in the ribs. 'You've got two planes coming in to land on one airstrip. Go out and play air-traffic controller.'

She glanced behind her at her mangled potatoes and she shrugged. 'I might as well come and see what's going on,' she added. 'Something tells me we're having an omelette for lunch anyway.'

The red plane landed first, with a smooth textbook landing, but even when the doors opened and the occupants emerged there was no clue as to their identity. A diminutive, elderly lady with sculpted white hair, expensively dressed in a smart crimson business suit, emerged from the passenger seat. Her pilot was a burly, seemingly impassive individual in a navy and white pilot's uniform. He helped the lady out and then stood back, as if in deference. A chauffeur?

The woman looked towards the house. She saw Riley and started towards him, but he waved her to stop. She was on the far side of the strip and she was forced to wait until the second plane came in to land.

The next plane didn't make such a smooth landing. The Holmes's plane was bigger and much, much older. In fact it looked like nothing so much as a tin can held together with baling twine. It hit the runway and squeaked, rattled and clanked to a shaky halt, its pilot hauling at the controls as if he was having trouble keeping the plane headed where he wanted.

The plane's elderly occupants—a man and a woman dressed in dilapidated farming gear—took their time to climb out, and when they did it seemed they were mid-domestic tirade.

'I told you we needed to get rid of this rust bucket.' The woman was scolding at full blast. 'We've got the money in the bank, you old skinflint. Regardless of what the girl and the kiddie do, we're taking this bucket of bolts down to Adelaide, and we don't come back until you've got us something respectable to fly in.' She looked across the strip and saw Riley and she waved wildly. 'Hey, Jackson.' Her hat fell off. She stopped to retrieve it. She gave her loose trousers a tug to make sure they stayed up and she headed straight for him.

Despite his confusion, Riley smiled. He'd met this pair before at the cattle sales. Bill and Dot were the couple who lived a hundred miles north of Barinya Downs, and Bill had been the one who'd contacted him about Jenna and Karli. He liked Dot a lot.

But what were they doing here? Dot was a plump, gregarious little country woman with a nose for good-humoured gossip, but Bill usually kept himself firmly to himself.

The well-dressed woman and her pilot had started walking towards him as well. He strolled across to meet them all—his four unlikely visitors.

Dot reached him first. 'Dot, it's great to see you,' he told her, smiling warmly down at the little woman. 'To what do I owe the pleasure?'

'We've come to take your visitors to Adelaide,' Dot told him, and she assumed an attitude of virtue that didn't quite gel with the glances of curiosity she was giving the lady in the suit. 'I told Bill it was the only Christian thing to do.'

'You mean you couldn't keep your nose out of what's not our business,' Bill said, exasperated, but he was smiling as well. He reached Riley and held out a hand in greeting. 'Hey, mate. We thought we'd rid you of your visitors. Or rather Dot thought we'd rid you of your visitors and I'm here under sufferance. We thought we'd take them to Adelaide for you.'

'But they've already gone,' Riley told him.

He didn't like saying it, he decided. He didn't like the way Dot's face fell in disappointment. It was too much an echo of how he felt himself. He turned to his other visitors to give himself time to make a recovery. 'I'm sorry.' He held out his hand to the lady in crimson. 'I'm afraid I don't know you. Should I?'

'I'm Enid O'Connell,' the lady told him, and she gripped his hand in a hold that was firmer than Bill's. Her face puckered in concern. 'Have I missed them?'

'You're looking for Jenna and Karli as well?'

'I am.' Then, as he looked confused she explained. 'I met them on the train. I was the one who instigated the search. The police told me they were here, but I couldn't stop worrying. I've done a bit of homework and managed to resolve a few of their problems, so I thought I'd fly out to put their minds at rest.'

His confusion didn't lessen one bit. 'How could you do that?'

'As it happens, it was easy.' She released his hand and looked up at him, her eyes assessing. He was doing his own assessing. What had Bill told him about the elderly lady on the train? Enid O'Connell? That she'd been a chief magistrate? Riley could understand how this lady could have held such a position. Her eyes were piercing, and her features spoke of a fierce intelligence. 'I took a really strong dislike to Brian,' she told him.

'I've never met Brian,' he said slowly as the rest of the group tried to take in what she was saying. 'But I feel the same way. Um…tell me again why you're here? You've resolved some of Jenna's problems? Tell me how.'

'The man's a petty thug,' Enid told him. 'But he chose the wrong people to be witness to his extraordinary outburst. We were stuck on the train for two days and there was such a mix of people on the passenger list. Before we reached Perth I'd found three lawyers, a judge, a criminal psychologist, a—'

'I think I've lost you,' Riley said. He looked around at Bill and Dot and Maggie and the pilot of Enid's plane and he could see she'd lost them as well. Or maybe not the pilot. The pilot was just plain impassive.

'It's easy,' Enid told them, obviously exasperated at minds that were less acute than hers. 'I was telling the little girl a story when Brian burst into the train's sitting room. Brian was shouting at the child, telling her he'd conned her out of her share of her mother's estate. Almost in the same breath, he was telling her that her mother was dead. The whole passenger lounge was appalled. Anyway, between us we had so many contacts that, with internet connections and phone calls, by the time we reached Perth we had the entire story. In fact, we had enough to go straight to court. We now have signed statements from no fewer than eight witnesses. Brian admitted he lied to get Karli and Jenna out of England, and it's now all so beautifully documented that he'll never get out of it.'

'He lied?' Maggie said blankly, and Enid nodded in satisfaction.

'The man's a fool. He was drunk, both with alcohol and with triumph, and he told the world how clever he'd been. Or how clever he thought he'd been. There were those among us who...well, who knew enough to encourage him. Anyway, the outcome is that there's no way Nicole's codicil can be overturned, as it's been manipulated by fraud. Brian's welcome to dispute it, but, as far as we can see, Nicole's will stands. The girls will inherit everything.'

That was something to think about. They'd be rich, Riley thought. They'd be independent. Strangely, it gave him no pleasure at all.

It should. He wanted them to be independent. Didn't he?

'So you arranged to fly all the way from Perth to tell them that.' Riley gazed at Enid in astonishment and she gazed back at him, her face serious.

'I had to. I kept thinking of those two white faces the last time I saw them and I thought Jenna must be frantic. When I heard she hadn't rejoined the train yesterday I thought, Dammit, I can afford it, so I'll get in a plane and come and tell them what's happening.'

Riley might be confused himself, but the rest of the group seemed just plain dumbfounded. 'That's…um…great,' Dot ventured. Riley's elderly neighbour clearly hadn't understood a word of what Enid had said, but Dot was examining Riley now and she seemed uncertain about the expression on his face—as well as confused by the story. 'Isn't it great? Do you think it's great, Riley?'

'Riley doesn't know what to think,' Maggie said shortly. 'He's in love with Jenna.'

The whole world stilled.

Gee, thanks, Maggie, Riley thought, but he didn't say it. He didn't know what to say.

The silence went on and on. The pup nosed in and licked Riley's hand. He whined softly as if he, too, was confused.

Everyone was confused.

Riley tried for anger, but it didn't work. He tried for disdain or amusement or…or anything.

Nothing worked.

'Riley's fallen in love with Nicole Razor's daughter?' Dot asked at last, and Maggie nodded.

'Hey, mate,' Bill managed. 'Whatcha go and do a thing like that for?'

'You mean what did he go and fall in love for?' Dot demanded, recovering a little and rounding on her husband. 'Why shouldn't he fall in love? Ooh. They must have got smitten while they were stuck at Barinya Downs. How romantic is that?'

'It's not even the slightest bit romantic,' her husband retorted. 'If you think Barinya Downs is romantic, you must have kangaroos loose in your top paddock.'

'Yeah, but if they fell in love there now… It's like you and me,' Dot said dreamily. 'I saw our place for the first time when we were in drought. You took me there and I thought it was great. I thought you were great. I fell in love then and you knew I was serious. Marriage is for the good times and the bad. If the bad times come first, then the marriage will last for ever.' She sniffed and groped for a handkerchief. 'So there. It *is* romantic.'

'Yeah, but he can't see it,' Maggie said obtusely. 'He thinks she'll walk out on him.'

'Why would she walk out on him?' Enid asked, and Riley decided it was time to intervene.

'Excuse me, but this is my—'

He was ignored.

'Because every woman who's ever come near this place has walked away,' Maggie was saying over the top of him. 'He reckons if he falls for

Jenna and they try and make a go of it, then it'll end in failure and the littlie'll be hurt.'

Bill frowned. 'That's a bit of a long shot.'

'You try telling him that,' Maggie retorted. 'He's got rocks in his head.'

'Will you butt out of what's not your business?' Riley demanded.

'I flew all the way from Perth,' Enid told him. 'It *is* my business.'

'And if we hadn't contacted you and told you the cops were looking for them, you'd have had a search party at Barinya Downs days ago and you never would have fallen in love,' Dot said severely. 'So it's our business, too.'

'I haven't fallen in love,' Riley snapped.

'Haven't you?' Maggie demanded. She fixed him with a look he'd first been fixed with when he was two years old. 'Can you look me in the eye, Riley Jackson, and tell me you don't love her? That you don't love the pair of them?'

He couldn't. Of course he couldn't.

He tried another track. 'Hell, I don't want to hurt them.'

'So what are you doing sending them away?'

'It wouldn't work. They'll get hurt.'

'They can't be hurt any more than they are now,' Maggie told him. 'They've fallen for you. Just look at Karli's rock. What sort of loving's that?'

He should dispute it. He should even manage to laugh.

Instead he dug Karli's rock from his pocket. He stared down at it while the misassorted group around him stared at him.

Hell.

They can't be hurt any more than they are now.

Karli was flying down to Adelaide without her rock.

Jenna was flying down to Adelaide—without him.

'I can't,' he said, and Maggie beamed.

'Yes, you can.'

He stared at Maggie and she stared back.

He gazed at Dot and Bill.

What had Dot said?

Marriage is for the good times and the bad. If the bad times come first, then the marriage will last for ever.

Jenna had fallen for him when they were at Barinya Downs. She'd said she loved him when they were in that damned awful swimming hole. She hadn't even known this place existed.

She'd said she loved him, knowing she had no money, thinking he had no money, believing Barinya Downs was the way he lived.

Maybe, he thought cautiously, just maybe, he'd been a fool.

Something shifted inside him right there. He waited for it to right itself, but it didn't. This was a fundamental shift, moving things back that had been first hauled out of place when his mother had left. They'd stayed out of place when his sisters had gone, his father had died, his wife had left.

And now they were back in place. They were back in place because of Jenna, and suddenly he knew absolutely and for sure that this shift was for ever.

'I don't have a plane,' he said blankly, and Maggie's mouth twitched at the corners. A smile started at the back of her worried eyes.

'I can see two.'

'We'll take you to Adelaide straight away.' Dot was also starting to smile. She was quick, was Dot. 'We're flying there anyway, and there's plenty of room in the back.'

Riley stared at her. Then he stared at the plane.

He turned to Enid. 'Enid…'

'Hey, you're not borrowing my plane,' Enid said. She could catch on fast as well. She grinned at her pilot, who gazed back in stolid indifference. 'It's only a two-seater and Harold and I are coming. We need to watch. Don't we, Harold?'

'Yes, ma'am.'

Riley glanced again at Dot and Bill's tin can with wings. 'We'll never catch them. Not in that.'

'I'll radio Max,' Maggie said serenely. 'I can have him do a few big loops so he loses an hour before landing. I bet he can do it without Jenna knowing a thing.' She glanced at Bill and Dot's plane and her smile deepened. 'Or maybe I should make that two hours. Lots of big loops.'

'Is it safe?' Riley demanded. He might be haring off on a mission of the heart, but he had no plans to get himself killed in the process.

'Of course it's safe,' Bill said, outraged. 'We've used it to transport a bit of blood and bone fertiliser, though. It might be a bit smelly in the back.'

'Oh, great.'

'Hey, what's a bit of fertiliser to a man in love?' Bill demanded, entering into the spirit of things. 'You want to win the lady or not?'

Riley gazed at all of them. They all gazed back.

He stared down at his stone.

He looked at the dog. *His* dog. The pup was nuzzling his hand, just as a much-loved dog had done all those years ago.

He'd call him Bustle, he thought, after a dog he used to know.

Maybe he could give this love business one more go.

No. Three more goes.

Bustle.

Karli.

Jenna.

'There's no saying she'll have me,' he warned, and Maggie's face cleared as if by magic.

'Oh, Riley, of course she'll have you. She loves you.'

'Of course she'll love you, young man,' Enid told him. 'If I didn't have Harold here, I'd love you myself. I haven't seen such excellent husband material going begging for a very long time. Now shake a leg. You're wasting time.'

'Faint heart never won fair lady,' Harold said—and everybody stared.

The statue had a voice.

Enid chuckled and reached out to hug her pilot. 'Well, you'd know,' she said, and Harold hugged her back.

'He's right,' Bill said. 'Faint heart, hey? You'd never want to be called that, now, would you, Jackson? Well. If you're brave enough to cope with a bit of blood and bone, then we're game enough to take you. Take a good sniff of decent air, young fella, cos it's the last clean air you'll smell until we get to Adelaide.' He gave a whoop that could be heard in the next state and headed back towards the plane. 'Let's get this baby in the air.'

'Baby,' Dot snorted heading after him. 'Demented geriatric, more like.'

'We'll need to refuel before we go,' Enid told them.

'Then do it,' Bill told her over his shoulder. 'You'll have to catch us up, though. We've got enough fuel on board and we're on a mission to Adelaide. One fair lady, coming up.'

'I'm crazy,' Riley said faintly, and Maggie shoved back his hat and planted a kiss on his forehead.

'No,' she said firmly. 'At last you're being sensible. After thirty-two years, you're finally seeing sense. Go, Riley, go. Bring your family home.'

CHAPTER ELEVEN

'THIS flight seems to be taking a very long time.' Jenna glanced at her watch. It had been almost three hours since they'd taken off from Munyering. She'd assumed Munyering was on the edge of viable grazing land, which surely meant that it wasn't too far from Adelaide.

'There's been a head wind,' Max called out over his shoulder. He'd been quiet for most of the trip, which had suited Jenna's mood. Every now and then he'd spoken briefly into his radio, but his voice had been too muted for her to hear what he'd been saying, and he'd made no move to engage her in conversation.

Karli had drifted into sleep, which had also fitted Jenna's bleak mood. She'd been free to stare out the window and think about everything she was leaving.

Everything she was facing.

'We're coming into Adelaide now,' Max called. 'Make sure the kiddy's seat belt's tight.'

'Can we get a flight on to Perth from here?' Jenna asked and Max shook his head.

'I'm flying you into Parafield, which is the run-way for private planes,' he told her. 'You'll need to catch a cab to the main airport to go to Perth.'

'I don't suppose you could radio ahead and see if there are any seats on commercial flights leaving this afternoon?' Jenna asked, and he shook his head again.

'I dunno how to do that.'

Great. Jenna bit her lip. She couldn't afford to spend a night in Adelaide.

'We're going down now,' Max told her. He glanced at his dials and bit his lip. 'I've spent as much time up here as I... I mean, I've been held up long enough. With the wind and everything. We're running low on fuel. Hold onto the kiddy.'

Sitting in Bill and Dot's cargo area wasn't the most comfortable way Riley had ever flown. In fact, it was the most uncomfortable ride he'd ever had.

And, beside him, Bill whinged all the time.

'If I'd thought I'd have ended up in the cargo hold I never would have come. Dot, hold this tank steady. I'll throw up if you bucket round any more.'

'That'll make the stink worse,' Dot called out from the pilot's seat. 'This tank doesn't know how to stay steady.'

'I offered to sit in the back.' Maggie was in the passenger seat, knitting and smiling and looking out at the scenery. Her last-minute decision to come was hardly surprising, Riley thought bitterly. Nothing about this day was surprising.

'You're not sitting in the back,' Dot retorted. 'I told you. It's not fit for ladies. It won't hurt Bill to see how awful it is. This way I might finally get a new plane.'

'Women.' Bill snorted. 'Are you sure you know what you're getting into, young fella?' He looked desperately over at Riley. 'Just say the word and we'll head back now.'

'We don't head back,' Riley said.

Parafield airport looked small and inconspicuous and incredibly lonely. Jenna helped Karli down from the plane. The air was totally still. Totally calm.

'What happened to the wind?' she asked.

'Upward currents,' Max said and he sounded a bit strained. 'Stratospheric conditions. Nimbus or something. You don't feel them under a thousand feet.'

'Oh.' She gave him a doubtful look. But there was nothing she could say. 'You've been really good to us,' she told Max. 'Thank you.'

Max cast a worried look up at the sky—checking nimbus? 'Yeah, well, there's no need to rush off. It'll take me a while to unload your gear.'

'There's only one suitcase each.'

'Yeah, but…there's customs and stuff.'

'Customs?'

'Yeah, well, fruit quarantine,' he said, a trifle desperately. 'Same thing as customs. There's laws about flying fruit from different areas and everything's got to be inspected. They've got beagle dogs, and the suitcases have to be sniffed before you're allowed out of the airport. You and the littlie wait in the lounge while I sort it out.'

'Can't we take the suitcases straight through?' The place looked empty.

'Rules is rules,' Max said doggedly, with another look upwards. 'I dunno where the dogs are. You go and sit down and I'll bring your stuff in as soon as it's cleared.'

There was another plane coming in to land, and as Jenna and Karli headed reluctantly indoors he chewed his bottom lip in dismay.

It was the wrong damned plane.

'How were we supposed to know the Minister for Agriculture was choosing today of all days to visit Adelaide?' Dot demanded. They'd been put into a circling pattern and Riley was going nuts. They were all going nuts. 'Heck, we'll be stuck up here for ever.'

'I'm going to die,' Bill said, clutching his stomach.

'Is there a parachute?' Riley demanded, but Dot just grinned and turned the plane into another wide circle.

Holding pattern.

Karli was miserable enough to complain, which, for Karli, was miserable indeed. 'Why is it taking so long to get our suitcases out of the plane?'

They'd sat in the waiting area as politicians had greeted politicians. It had taken for ever, and no one had done anything about the woman and child patiently waiting for Max's phantom dog-fruit-checkers to appear. Max himself was nowhere to be seen. Finally, as the dignitaries left in a fleet of chauffeur-driven limousines even Karli voiced her impatience.

Enough, Jenna thought. Enough.

'I have no idea, but, fruit or no fruit, dogs or no dogs, I'm getting them now,' she said. 'Come on, Karli.'

She walked to the door, she swung it wide—and Riley was on the other side.

*   *   *

She was still here.

Riley had been stuck in the air for an hour waiting for clearance to land, and he had visions of Jenna catching a cab to the main airport and getting a plane straight away to Perth and…

He shoved open the terminal door and she was right in front of him.

'Riley.'

She said his name and the world righted itself

She was here.

She sounded stupid. She felt stupid. The world was falling away, and for a moment she thought she might faint.

But two strong hands came out and caught her and held her steady.

'You're here.' Riley sounded as stunned as she felt.

'Of course we're here,' she managed, and then she tried to think what next to say. 'They think we have fruit.'

'Fruit,' Riley said blankly. 'What sort of fruit?'

'I have no idea.'

'Max says people stick bananas in their luggage, and he's gone to find the dogs to sniff them out,' Karli ventured. Jenna might be too stunned to think straight, but Karli was just plain pleased. 'Hello,

Riley,' she said. 'Can you tell the man with the dogs that I ate my banana on the way and it's silly that we have to wait and wait. Why are you here?'

'I came to find you,' Riley told her. He wasn't looking at Karli, though. He was looking at Jenna. He was holding onto Jenna. 'I had to bring you your rock.'

'I left the rock for you,' Karli said.

'It was your gift.'

'But you need it.'

'I don't need it,' Riley said, and his grip on Jenna grew tighter. 'I have you.'

Silence.

They were blocking the door. Karli was behind Jenna on one side of the door. Enid and Harold and Dot and Bill and Maggie were behind Riley on the other side of the door.

It was a less-than-desirable position for all of them. Enid and Harold and Dot and Bill and Maggie couldn't see.

'Do something, Harold,' Enid ordered, so Harold put his shoulder to the door and pushed, propelling Jenna and Riley back into the waiting area. He propelled them so hard that Jenna almost fell over.

She couldn't fall. Riley had her tight and he wasn't letting go.

The others tumbled inside.

'Has he kissed her yet?' Dot demanded of Karli, and Karli looked confused.

'No.'

'What's he waiting for, then?' Dot demanded, and Jenna tried to haul herself away—but not very hard. She tried to make some sense of what was happening. 'Who...?'

'These are Dot and Bill, our neighbours at Barinya Downs,' Riley told her, but his eyes didn't leave hers. His hands were tight on her waist, and he was looking down at her with an expression that made her heart twist. That made her world twist. 'You know Maggie, of course. Good old interfering Maggie. And this is Enid, who I gather you met on the train. Oh, and Harold who's her...her...'

'Her lover,' Enid finished briskly, taking right over from a man who was clearly incompetent to explain anything. 'Jenna, we've fixed up that business about the will. You and Karli now should inherit all your mother's money. I gather there's a lot. You stand to be very wealthy women.'

She'd be a wealthy woman. Harold was Enid's lover. Maggie was here.

Riley had Karli's rock.

It was all very confusing. She should think about all these things, Jenna decided. She couldn't.

Nothing mattered except the way Riley was looking at her and the feel of his hands on her waist and…

'Why are you here?' she whispered and his hands tightened still further.

'Because I've been a fool.'

'Yeah, that's a good reason to sit in a cargo hold full of fertiliser for three hours,' Bill retorted. 'You've done that because you've *been* a fool? You're going to have to do better than that.'

'Because I love you?' Riley said.

That was better. Everybody seemed to think that was better.

Especially Jenna. Jenna let herself look up into Riley's face and what she saw there was very, very satisfactory indeed.

'Really?' she asked.

'Really,' he said.

'But how can you love me? You don't even like your dog.'

'If Bustle could have fitted in the cargo hold he'd be here right now,' Riley told her. His eyes didn't leave hers and his smile was making her heart perform cartwheels. 'I love my stupid dog. I've fallen really hard for a cute little button of a kid called Karli. But most of all, I've fallen for you, Jenna Svenson. I've fallen so hard I don't think I can ever recover. I've been a dope. But between them, these guys have made me see sense. And you've made me see sense. My wonderful, darling Jenna.'

She took a deep breath. She searched his face for evidence that he was joking.

She forgot about breathing entirely.

'Really?' she whispered.

'Nope,' he told her, smiling that gorgeous, heart-stopping smile before he hauled her into him again to hold her hard against his chest. 'But Enid tells me you're a very wealthy woman and I'm a gold-digger from way back.'

She ignored the superfluous and concentrated on the necessary. 'You love me?'

He stopped smiling. He held her away from him—just a little—so that she could look into his eyes and see exactly what was in his heart.

'I do,' he said softly. 'I love the way you look. I love the way you smile. I love your spirit and your courage and the way you look when you tie your hair in rags and you have dust on your nose. I love the way you giggle and the way you hold Karli and I love the way you face life with so much courage and with so much love. Jenna, I can't be-lieve that you could possibly love me, but you told me—back there in the waterhole—that you could love me. I want to know if I've blown it. I need to know if I've stuffed it entirely or if I've got a chance. If...'

He could go no further. She'd stood on tiptoes and her lips had reached his.

'Oh, Riley,' she whispered 'Oh, Riley, my love. How can you doubt it?'

He kissed her. He kissed her then as she deserved to be kissed. As she needed to be kissed. As she'd wanted to be kissed for ever and for ever but she'd never known it—because how could a girl know that a kiss could feel like this? That a body against hers could feel this good? That two hearts could merge into one just like this?

He kissed her and kissed her and kissed her—and then the tables turned and she kissed him right back.

Over and over.

Life started—until death did them part. It started right there. When finally they pulled away from each other, the rest of their lives had already begun.

'Yuk,' said Karli.

'Don't you like kissing?' Maggie was smiling and smiling.

'No,' Karli retorted. 'But I said yuk 'cos Riley smells disgusting.'

'So does Bill,' Dot said cheerfully. 'But still I love him.' She looked doubtfully at her disreputable husband. 'Or I think I do. Mostly. As long as he buys us a new aeroplane.' Then she turned back to Karli. 'You know, if Jenna's kissing Riley when he smells as bad as he does now, then it's definitely serious.'

'You mean they might get married?'

'Of course they're getting married,' Enid said briskly. 'I'm qualified to perform a marriage ceremony and there are at least seventy people I know from a certain train ride who are just aching for an invitation.'

'Oh, I'll be able to plan the best wedding at Munyering,' Maggie said dreamily.

'What about having it at Barinya Downs?' Dot retorted. 'That's where it all started.' She grinned. 'We could have a waterside ceremony by that awful dam on Riley's place. Now there's romance for you.'

'It'd be cheap,' Bill said reflectively. 'There's always that.'

'Yeah, we could feed all the guests baked beans and beer,' Maggie retorted. 'A wedding with a difference. I don't think so.'

'Can I be a flower girl?' Karli asked, and Maggie hauled her up into her arms and hugged. Maggie's role as Grandma-elect was about to start right now.

'Of course you can be.' She beamed. 'We'll make you the prettiest dress. All pink and white with a huge pink bow.'

'But what would a wealthy woman like Jenna do at Munyering?' Enid asked thoughtfully. Her forte, it seemed, was planning for the future.

'She's a nurse,' Maggie said. 'Jenna could run the remote clinics for the Flying Doctor. They'd think that was great. And Karli could do School of the Air. We could have such fun.'

'They'd both have to learn to ride a horse,' Dot added. 'I could help there. I've got a couple of quiet old nags I could let you have, Jenna, and it'd be great to have another woman to help with the muster.'

'Hey, Jenna, you could learn to fly,' Bill said, catching the spirit of the future and joining in with enthusiasm. 'Then you'd need another plane so you can go shopping in Adelaide any time you want. What with all your money and that. And...' he assumed an air of innocent nonchalance '...I just happen to know where you can get a really reliable plane at a very reasonable price. One owner from new.'

'Yeah, right, only driven by a little old lady to church on Sundays,' Dot said dryly and Jenna choked.

'But he hasn't asked her to marry him yet,' Harold observed, and they stilled.

'Neither he has,' Bill said. 'There's still a chance, mate. Ouch!' Dot jabbed him hard in the ribs and he shifted sideways and looked wounded. But then he grinned.

'You are going to, aren't you, Riley?' Maggie asked.

'Indeed you must,' Enid said. 'You don't get an offer of a free marriage celebrant every day of the week.'

'Will you marry Jenna?' Karli asked.

There was a note of panic in her voice. It was a sudden jolt that stopped the laughter. Karli knew this world was serious. She knew good things didn't necessarily happen.

Life was tough and happy endings were for story books.

But life wasn't too tough. Not here. Not now.

'You know, it seems to me that bad things have happened to us in the past,' Riley said seriously. He let Jenna go—with reluctance—and lifted Karli from Maggie's into his own arms. He held her and smiled at her and Jenna felt her heart twist all over again. 'Your mum died,' he said softly. 'Jenna and I have been lonely. There's been bad stuff. But good things happen, too. So it seems to me that we've done our bad stuff. We've been lonely for long enough. It's time we had the good stuff.'

'The happy ending,' she said, echoing Jenna's thoughts.

'No,' Riley told her. 'No happy endings. I don't like happy endings.'

'What do you like?' Karli whispered.

'How about happy beginnings? What do you think about that?'

'I think I like them,' she said seriously, thinking about it. As a concept it seemed pretty good. 'Happy beginnings. You and me and Jenna and Maggie and your puppy.'

'It's a ready-made family,' Riley told her. 'As soon as Jenna agrees to marry me.'

'Will you marry him?' Karli asked and turned to face her.

Would she marry him?

'I would,' Enid said. 'Marriage is a very sensible arrangement.'

'Hey, that means you ought to marry me,' said Harold.

'Give me Karli,' Maggie ordered, and lifted Karli back so that Riley had a clear track to Jenna. 'Ask her again.'

'Think carefully,' Bill said.

'What's there to think about, stinky?' Dot demanded and hugged her husband.

What was there to think about?

Nothing. Not very much.

Riley smiled and smiled. Then, realising that the entire world was watching—the whole disreputable cast of this comedy of manners, plus the entire terminal staff—he rose to the occasion.

Or, rather, he dropped to the occasion. He fell to one knee.

'Will you marry me, Jenna Svenson?' he asked.

And what was a girl to say to that?

'Yes,' she said promptly, and she fell to her knees as well. 'Yes, I will.'

There was simply no other answer to give.

MILLS & BOON® PUBLISH EIGHT LARGE PRINT TITLES A MONTH. THESE ARE THE EIGHT TITLES FOR DECEMBER 2005

THE GREEK'S BOUGHT WIFE
Helen Bianchin

BEDDING HIS VIRGIN MISTRESS
Penny Jordan

HIS WEDDING-NIGHT HEIR
Sara Craven

THE SICILIAN'S DEFIANT MISTRESS
Jane Porter

THE OUTBACK ENGAGEMENT
Margaret Way

RESCUED BY A MILLIONAIRE
Marion Lennox

A FAMILY TO BELONG TO
Natasha Oakley

PARENTS OF CONVENIENCE
Jennie Adams

MILLS & BOON®

Live the emotion

1105 Rom LP

MILLS & BOON® PUBLISH EIGHT LARGE PRINT TITLES A MONTH. THESE ARE THE EIGHT TITLES FOR JANUARY 2006

———— ❧ ————

THE RAMIREZ BRIDE
Emma Darcy

EXPOSED: THE SHEIKH'S MISTRESS
Sharon Kendrick

THE SICILIAN MARRIAGE
Sandra Marton

AT THE FRENCH BARON'S BIDDING
Fiona Hood-Stewart

THEIR NEW-FOUND FAMILY
Rebecca Winters

THE BILLIONAIRE'S BRIDE
Jackie Braun

CONTRACTED: CORPORATE WIFE
Jessica Hart

IMPOSSIBLY PREGNANT
Nicola Marsh

MILLS & BOON®

Live the emotion

1205 Rom